A Roman Shadow

A Roman Shadow

A Chief Inspector Shadow Mystery

H L Marsay

TULE
PUBLISHING

DEDICATION

For J,
With love x

Acknowledgements

My thanks to the magnificent team at Tule: Jane Porter, Meghan Farrell, Cyndi Parent and Nikki Babri.

I was so lucky to work with three amazing editors on this book: Sinclair Sawhney, Helena Newton and Marlene Roberts. Many thanks for all your suggestions and your patience.

Thanks also to Patrick Knowles for another wonderful book cover and to Lee Hyat for coordinating the design.

CHAPTER ONE

Down 7.
Will Mum use this building to inspire and educate? (6 letters)

DETECTIVE CHIEF INSPECTOR John Shadow placed his knife and fork together and pushed the now empty plate to one side as he swallowed down the last mouthful of bacon. His full English breakfast in Bettys had been as delicious as always. He was sitting at his usual corner table from where he could quietly observe his fellow customers. The famous tearooms were particularly busy this morning. There was an influx of Chinese visitors to the city, all here to celebrate the beginning of their New Year. He watched as they used their phones to take photos of each other and the Bettys waitresses in their traditional black and white uniforms, who patiently paused to pose with their guests.

A hint of a smile flickered across Shadow's face. He was quite content to observe other people and how they interacted, just as long as nobody tried to interact with him.

As the staff hurried back and forth, Shadow realised he hadn't seen Julie, his regular waitress, for almost two weeks. Was she ill? Maybe she'd changed shifts. If she had any sense, she would be on holiday abroad enjoying some winter sun and escaping the cold and damp of York in February. As he mused to himself, it didn't cross his mind to ask any of Julie's colleagues where she was.

However, he did notice the single red roses discreetly placed in vases on each table. A warning that Valentine's Day was imminent. He sighed and made a mental note to avoid the Italian restaurants he frequented most evenings on that particular date. It was over twenty-five years since he'd celebrated Valentine's and now the thought of being sur-rounded by adoring couples staring into each other's eyes filled him with dread.

A quick glance at his watch told him he had ten minutes to complete the *Yorkshire Post* crossword before he was due at the Eboracum Museum. The previous evening, as he was about to leave his office, he had received a phone call from the director of the museum asking him to visit at his earliest convenience. The gentleman wouldn't explain why over the telephone, but he had sounded quite agitated.

A LITTLE OVER ten minutes later and with six down still eluding him, Shadow reluctantly folded his copy of the *Yorkshire Post* and tucked it into the deep pocket of his old wax jacket. He stepped outside into the bitterly cold Febru-ary air. On the other side of St Helen's Square, his sergeant,

Jimmy Chang, was already waiting for him outside the police station. As usual he was dressed in jeans, trainers and a black leather jacket, but today he also had a long black and red scarf wound around his neck. His young colleague was not a fan of cold weather.

"Good morning, Sergeant. I wasn't expecting you to be this eager to pay a visit to the museum," said Shadow as the two detectives fell into step together.

"Morning, Chief. Actually, on our way over there I wanted to ask if I could pick your brains about something?"

"No," replied Shadow instinctively, "not if it's about a Valentine's present for Sophie. I've only just recovered from the whole Christmas debacle."

Jimmy's girlfriend was Dr Sophie Newton, one of the pathologists they worked with. Since the start of their relationship, Shadow had found himself the unwilling sounding board for every romantic gesture or purchase Jimmy was considering. When Jimmy had heard about the old tradition of giving gifts for the twelve days after Christmas that inspired the carol of the same name, he had very nearly driven his boss insane with his constant chatter as he tried to find a dozen appropriate presents.

"No, it's nothing like that," replied Jimmy, "although I have been giving it a lot of thought. I spent ages browsing around the shops at the weekend. I'm definitely going to get some of those handmade liqueur chocolates she likes from that place on Swinegate, but then I wanted to give her something to celebrate Chinese New Year too, you know with them falling on the same weekend."

Shadow groaned loudly.

"It's okay though, like I said I've been giving it a lot of thought and I've almost made a decision."

"Then I'm thrilled for both of us."

"But that's not what I wanted to ask you about. You see Sophie's brothers have asked me to play in a charity rugby match they're organising."

"Say no!" advised Shadow immediately. He gave a slight shudder. Rugby had been compulsory at his boarding school. Five years of being crushed in scrums and tackled to the cold, wet, muddy ground by an opposition player, who always seemed to weigh over sixteen stone, had put him off the game for life.

"I can't do that, Chief; they already think I'm a bit weird because I don't drink bitter or watch football."

"I'm telling you now, you'll regret it." He looked his sergeant's long lanky frame up and down. "In fact I'll be amazed if you don't end up in traction."

"Sophie's brothers are both big rugby fans and I really want to try to bond with them."

Shadow had briefly met Sophie's parents and two younger brothers over Christmas when Rose, Jimmy's mother, had hosted a special dinner for them all. Shadow had ducked out of the dinner but had stopped by for a drink. Henry and James were both strapping young men from the north-east with Sophie's easy-going nature and fondness for a pint or three. He now recalled one had a broken nose and the other cauliflower ears.

"Didn't you play rugby at school?" he asked. Jimmy shook his head.

"No, only football, and to be honest I was more into athletics. I don't even know how many players are on a team."

"It depends—is it rugby union or league?"

"I don't know. What's the difference?"

"Thirteen players for league and fifteen for union," explained Shadow as Jimmy quickly started to make notes. Shadow sighed. "Look, tell them you'll play on the wing and if anyone throws you the ball, catch it and run like hell."

They paused for a moment and waited for the traffic lights on the corner of St Leonard's Place to change before they crossed the road.

"What does Sophie make of all this?" Shadow asked. Jimmy's girlfriend tended to be the more pragmatic one of the couple. He couldn't think she would approve of the idea that her boyfriend was likely to be flattened by a seventeen-stone hooker.

"Oh, I haven't really spoken to her about it. She's really busy with work. Donaldson's disappeared to his place in the Algarve for a month, so she's got her hands full," Jimmy replied, referring to the other obnoxious and far less helpful pathologist they worked with.

"That's just our luck!" Shadow tutted. "Donaldson's

away and we can't take advantage of it because we don't have a murder to investigate."

Fortunately for Shadow they arrived at the museum before Jimmy could ask him for any more rugby-related tips. The Eboracum Museum was an elegant white building with an imposing portico and columns at the entrance. It stood on Exhibition Square, opposite the York Theatre Royal, next to the York Art Gallery and the rear elevation overlooked the Museum Gardens. The Victorians had built it to house the collection of Roman artefacts they started unearthing as York's rapid expansion in the 1800s led to more and more building work. Eboracum was the name the Romans gave to York when it was one of the most northerly cities in their empire. A fort was built where the Minster now stood to support the soldiers who were on their way to defend the border against the marauding tribes of Scots. A settlement soon sprang up around the garrison and became the basis of the city that stood there today.

THE MUSEUM DIDN'T open until ten o'clock, but Tim Dunnington, the museum director, was waiting to greet them at the door. He was a man of about fifty, medium height and slightly overweight. His dark hair was swept back and greying slightly at the temples. With his sombre, dark, three-piece suit he wore a tie that was both loud in its colour and abstract design.

"Ah there you are, Shadow, good of you to come. You too, Sergeant." He checked outside as he ushered them through the door. "Excellent, no flashing lights or sirens either. Let's try and keep everything on the QT shall we, chaps? Hush, hush and all that."

"What exactly is the problem?" enquired Shadow as the museum's door shut behind him with a loud thud. Dunnington reminded him of someone, but he couldn't recall who.

"Follow me to my office and I'll give you a sitrep," replied the director, who was already striding away. The two detectives followed Dunnington, through the museum. Their footsteps echoed around the empty atrium, as they walked briskly across the marble floor past tall columns and glass display cases holding carefully lit artefacts.

Mr Dunnington's office was at the end of a long corridor lined with mannequins dressed as different types of Roman gladiators. He opened the door and Shadow and Jimmy followed him inside. It was a large room painted white with a high ceiling and long windows overlooking Museum Gardens. Prints of the Colosseum and the Forum lined the wall. In front of the pale wood desk were several modern metal and light wood chairs. Two of these chairs were already occupied.

Shadow recognised Dr Stather immediately. He was the head archaeologist at York's Historic Foundation. The previous year he had briefly been one of the suspects in a murder investigation. Shadow had found him to be arrogant, pompous and a terrible liar. The two men nodded silently at each other in recognition. Sitting on the chair next to Stather was a lady dressed in a tweed skirt and jacket. Her grey hair was worn in a long plait down her back and she was sobbing quietly into a large white handkerchief.

Tim Dunnington invited the two detectives to sit down as he took his own seat behind the desk. Shadow noted that neither Dunnington nor Stather were making any attempt to comfort the crying woman. The museum director cleared his throat and folded his hands firmly in front of him before speaking.

"Chief Inspector Shadow, Sergeant Chang, may I introduce Dr Richard Stather who sits with me on the museum's board of trustees and Dr Dorothy Shepherd. Dorothy is the curator here. For heaven's sake, pull yourself together Dorothy," he snapped.

"Dr Stather and I have already met," replied Shadow. Tim Dunnington looked a little surprised, but Shadow didn't elaborate as Stather shifted uncomfortably in his chair. Shadow held out his hand to the lady who was trying her best to stop sobbing. "I'm pleased to meet you, Dr Shepherd."

The lady gave him a weak smile and a very damp hand-shake accompanied by several loud sniffs as she tried to stifle her tears. Dunnington cleared his throat again.

"Chief Inspector, I'll get straight to the point. The reason I asked you to come here is because several of the museum's artefacts have been stolen."

"I'm very sorry to hear that, Mr Dunnington. When did the theft occur?" asked Shadow as Jimmy switched on his electronic notebook, his finger poised ready to take down the relevant information. Tim Dunnington sighed and shot Dr Shepherd a furious look.

"That's just it, Chief Inspector, we don't know when or exactly what was taken. We are still carrying out our own investigations."

Shadow and Jimmy exchanged a puzzled glance.

"I don't quite follow," said the chief inspector.

"Allow me to give you a quick recap," replied Dunnington, settling back in his own large leather chair. "A couple of weeks ago, I was approached by the director of a museum in Colchester asking if we would loan him some pieces for an exhibition he was organising, focusing on Roman coins. I consulted Dr Stather and the other board members and we were all in agreement that we should accept this request."

Dr Stather nodded his head vigorously to confirm what the director was saying as Dunnington carried on.

"The exhibition was to begin in Colchester then travel around the country, stopping at other towns and cities founded by the Romans. York obviously, St Albans, Winchester and Chester, before completing the tour of duty at the British Museum."

"Sorry," interrupted Jimmy, "was that Winchester and Chester?"

Dr Shepherd, who was sitting next to him leaned over to look at his screen.

"Yes, Sergeant, that's right—both cities. Anywhere that ends in *chester* or *caster* or indeed *cester* was named by the Romans," she explained in a clear but slightly trembling voice.

"Thank you, Dorothy," snapped Dunnington again glaring at the curator. Dr Shepherd dropped her head and began twisting the handkerchief around her fingers. "As I was saying, the tour was planned; the pieces from our collection that were to be included were discussed and agreed upon. Representatives from Colchester Museum arrived two days ago and assessed the chosen artefacts for the purpose of their insurance." The director paused and glared even more fiercely at Dr Shepherd. "It was then that they informed us our pieces were not genuine but extremely good fakes. It was incredibly embarrassing not only for myself, you understand, but the whole museum. It has raised a great many questions about how the collection has been managed."

"Absolutely. Quite shocking," murmured Dr Stather in agreement. Shadow glanced between the two men. He might not yet understand all the details of this crime, but he understood Stather and Dunnington's response to it. They wanted to ensure Dr Shepherd took the blame whether she was responsible or not. If they couldn't prove she was guilty they wanted to show she was incompetent. From telling her to pull herself together to calling her by her first name even though she deserved the same title as Stather, they were undermining her. The two men were ganging up on Dr Shepherd and Shadow didn't like it. He turned his attention to the curator.

"Dr Shepherd, please could you tell me where the pieces in question came from? Were they bought at an auction or acquired from another collection?"

Dr Shepherd sat up straight in her chair and took a deep breath as she composed herself.

"No, Chief Inspector. All the pieces were discovered here in York. I unearthed several of them myself. You may remember almost two years ago there was an excavation close to The Mount. A contractor at one of the hotels was digging to make a swimming pool and inadvertently stumbled across the remains of a Roman nobleman's villa."

Shadow nodded. He certainly remembered the traffic chaos that was caused when one of the city's main roads was being dug up for several weeks. Dr Shepherd continued to explain.

"It turned out to be quite an important find. Not only did we discover one of the best-preserved mosaics in England, but some extremely rare coins and exquisite pieces of jewellery. Dr Stather and I both agreed it was one of the most exciting digs we had been lucky enough to work on."

Shadow turned to the archaeologist with an enquiring look and Stather's face reddened as he gave a curt nod. The chief inspector noted that Stather had yet to speak to him directly.

"So are you saying the genuine pieces you discovered have been replaced with replicas?"

"What other explanation is there, Chief Inspector?" interrupted Dunnington impatiently.

"And you have no idea when this exchange took place?"

"The insurance company sends a chap to assess and evaluate our collection every year. The last inspection was nine months ago. He didn't find anything untoward, so we can only assume it occurred after his visit."

"Have there been any break-ins or attempted burglars, anything suspicious during the last year?"

"No nothing at all. We have a state-of-the-art security system. It's absolutely tip-top and regularly maintained. I can assure you everything is quite in order."

Shadow nodded although he privately thought it was quite clear everything was not in order if part of the museum's collection had been replaced with replicas without anyone noticing. He stood up awkwardly, relieved to leave the modern metal-framed chair behind. It was every bit as uncomfortable as it looked.

"Perhaps Dr Shepherd would be good enough to show us

the pieces in question and we can begin to make some enquiries," he said. The curator stood up and Dunnington bristled slightly.

"I must ask you to be as discreet as possible, Chief Inspector. If this were to become public knowledge the reputation of our museum will be ruined."

"We'll do everything we can, Mr Dunnington," Shadow replied as he nodded to both Dunnington and Stather.

The two detectives followed Dr Shepherd out of the director's office and back down the corridor past the gladiator mannequins. Jimmy gestured towards them as they passed.

"These are great, Dr Shepherd," he said.

"Yes, we find they are very popular with visiting school children, Sergeant," she replied, pausing briefly. "I like to tell them how the retiarius, the one with the net and trident, would fight against the secutor, the chap standing next to him with the large shield and dagger. They love to hear all the gory details."

"Were there gladiators around in Roman York, Dr Shepherd?" asked Jimmy.

"Oh yes we believe so," replied the doctor with a small smile. "A settlement the size of Eboracum was sure to have had gladiatorial games to entertain the residents and the soldiers who were garrisoned here. Unfortunately we haven't yet found the site of the amphitheatre, but as ever I live in hope."

Shadow thought how much more relaxed Dr Shepherd

seemed since leaving her two colleagues behind. They were now back to the main atrium. A cleaner and two of the museum guides were preparing for opening time. Dr Shepherd greeted them each politely by name as she led Shadow and Jimmy up the wide, elegant stone staircase.

"How many people work here at the museum, Dr Shepherd?" asked Shadow, who was trying to discreetly locate an indigestion tablet in his coat pocket. He was concerned the growing noise of his grumbling stomach would soon be loud enough to echo around the place.

"Eighteen in total, but most are volunteers and almost all are only part-time, Chief Inspector. We are a small but happy bunch," she said brightly, then her face fell. "At least we usually are."

"Would I be able to have a list of everyone's name and how long they have been working here?"

"Of course. I'm sure Stephanie will be able to provide you with one—she's Mr Dunnington's secretary."

At the top of the stairs, three corridors led off in different directions. The one leading to the left had large gold letters above that read 'The Dunnington Wing'.

"I see the museum's director has a wing named after him," remarked Jimmy.

"Not the current Mr Dunnington, Sergeant, but his great-great-grandfather. Nathanial Dunnington was one of the founders of the museum. It was when they were excavating the land to build the railway station that the first Roman treasures were discovered. Fortunately, a few forward-thinking local businessmen had them preserved and raised enough funds to build this marvellous place. I am afraid we aren't heading down there though. I'm taking you to what I call the working corridor."

She turned and led them past a door marked 'Staff Room' and then paused outside one with a sign that read 'Director's Secretary'. She knocked and waited briefly before opening the door and poking her head inside.

"Oh dear, she must have popped out," she said closing the door once more. Next to the secretary's office was the storeroom. Dr Shepherd unlocked the door and led them inside.

"Is this room always locked?" asked Shadow.

"Yes, Chief Inspector, and only I and Mr Dunnington have a key," replied the curator.

The three of them stepped inside the storeroom. There was a large window overlooking Museum Gardens, a dark wood rectangular table in the middle of the room and the walls were lined from floor to ceiling with neatly labelled drawers. One of these drawers had a red x taped on it, as if it was somehow contaminated. Dr Shepherd pulled it open with a small sigh.

"These are the pieces that the Colchester team found to be fakes," she said carefully lifting the drawer out and placing it on the table. The drawer was divided into compartments. Shadow and Jimmy peered inside. Each compartment contained a gold coin with the head of what Shadow assumed was a Roman emperor. Some showed a wolf and two children. Shadow quickly calculated there were twenty coins. There was also one compartment containing a large gold ring set with a red stone.

"Is it okay if I take pictures of them, Dr Shepherd?" asked Jimmy pulling his mobile phone out of his pocket.

"Certainly, Sergeant; allow me to assist you," replied Dr Shepherd, who promptly retrieved a pair of white gloves from another drawer, slipped them on and held up each piece for Jimmy to photograph. "This coin shows the image of Constantine the Great and dates from around 327 AD. The next is a copy of a gold Solidus of Honorius and shows the last Roman emperor of Britain. He was famous of course for writing the *Rescript of Honorius*, basically asking the Britons to fend for themselves."

While they were busy, Shadow stepped over to the window and peered out. There was a good view of the ruins of St Mary's Abbey and the rest of Museum Gardens. Beneath the window and running the full width of the building was a long narrow ledge no more than eight inches wide. Many buildings in the area of a similar age had them. Estate agents optimistically described them as balconies, but they were really only wide enough to hold a plant pot. Down below on the ground were metal chairs and tables stacked in neat piles. Shadow assumed in good weather it was the outdoor seating area of the museum café. There was a lock on the window and an electric cable running into the woodwork, presumably for an alarm. It looked a little old-fashioned but didn't appear to have been damaged.

"Some of these are really pretty," he heard Jimmy saying to Dr Shepherd. "I like the one with the wolf and the babies."

"Ah yes the she-wolf suckling Romulus and Remus: the symbol of Rome."

"And this ring is nice too."

"We believe it belonged to the wife of the nobleman whose villa we excavated. Oh, if only you could have seen the originals, Sergeant Chang. Do you know much about antiquities or jewellery?" Dr Shepherd asked politely.

"Not really," replied Jimmy. "I'm just looking for inspiration for a present for my girlfriend. You know with Valentine's Day coming up."

Reflected in the glass of the window Shadow could see Dr Shepherd smiling indulgently at Jimmy. He rolled his eyes and tutted quietly to himself. Trust Jimmy to veer away from the investigation less than half an hour after it had begun.

"What a lovely idea! And how apt—after all St Valentine was said to be a Christian priest in Roman times," commented Dr Shepherd.

"Really?" asked Jimmy. Having worked with his sergeant for over a year now, Shadow was no longer surprised at his shaky grasp of history.

"Oh yes in the third century I believe. It's said he conducted some of the earliest Christian marriage ceremonies. Quite a dangerous occupation in those days, Sergeant."

Shadow turned away from the window. He'd heard enough. As interesting and well informed as Dr Shepherd might be, learning about St Valentine was not going to help them find the missing coins.

"Were the genuine coins always stored in here, Dr Shepherd?" he asked as Jimmy photographed the last piece.

"No, Chief Inspector. We have more artefacts than we have room to exhibit, so every couple of months we rotate them. That way our regular visitors have something new to look at."

"I see. Does that mean the theft could have taken place from either up here or from one of the public areas?"

"Yes, that's also why we can't tell you when the theft occurred. Although I decide which pieces are to be rotated, it is often one of the assistants who actually handles the pieces during the changeover and places them in the display cabinets while I supervise. It is quite possible they didn't notice there had been a switch. At first glance, these are very good copies and of course nobody had any reason to think they weren't the real thing. Perhaps if I had done it myself, well I like to think I would have noticed." Her voice trailed away and she paused for a second before giving her head a small shake. "Everything currently on display is genuine, but some of the other pieces here in storage—" she gestured to the drawers around her "—still need to be checked. Mr Dunnington has put Dr Stather in charge of that process."

Shadow could hear the hurt in her voice. It was obvious she was upset not to have been trusted to carry out the task.

"One last question: is it only yourself and Mr Dunnington who have keys to the exhibition cases downstairs too?"

"Yes, just the two of us," confirmed Dr Shepherd.

WHEN THE DETECTIVES and curator stepped back out into the corridor, they found two burly young men dressed as Roman soldiers complete with sandals, short leather tunics, red capes and gleaming helmets. They were chatting to a young woman with long blonde hair who looked to be in her early twenties. She was wearing a short black skirt, a tight-fitting cream silk blouse and she was giggling at something one of the soldiers had just said. All three turned around when they heard the storeroom door close.

"Morning, Dr Shepherd; all right, gents," said the Roman closest to them in a strong Essex accent.

"Good morning, Peter. Good morning, Glenn. Ah, Stephanie, there you are," said Dr Shepherd. The blonde turned and flushed a little as she flicked her hair away from her face.

"Were you looking for me, Dorothy?" she asked giving Shadow and Jimmy a sidelong glance.

"This is Chief Inspector Shadow and Sergeant Chang. They are here about…" Dr Shepherd paused and glanced at the two Roman soldiers. "I said you would be able to provide them with an up-to-date staff list."

"Well I suppose so. I've probably got one somewhere," Stephanie replied, folding her arms and tossing her head back.

"We'll catch you later then, Steph," said the other Roman. Shadow thought this one sounded as if he came from the West Midlands. The two soldiers headed down the corridor, their leather sandals slapping against the floor.

"Okay. Bye, Pete; see you later, Glenn," trilled Stephanie before turning back to Shadow with a sulky pout. "Do you want the list now?"

"If it's not too much trouble. I'd also like a floor plan of the museum and details of who installed the security system—and the insurance company too please."

Stephanie rolled her eyes and exhaled dramatically.

"Blimey, you don't want much do you?"

"Stephanie," chided Dr Shepherd gently, "the chief inspector is here to help."

"All right, all right, don't you start. For God's sake all this fuss for a few old coins," she snapped and with another toss of her long blonde hair she marched into her office, slamming the door behind her. Following her departure Dr Shepherd and the two detectives stood for a moment in awkward silence.

"Has Stephanie been Mr Dunnington's secretary for long?" enquired Shadow.

Dr Shepherd flushed a little. "About eighteen months, Chief Inspector." She paused. "And for six of those months she has also been the second Mrs Dunnington."

Shadow tried not to look surprised at the news that the pouting young blonde was married to the much older and seemingly rather stuffy Tim Dunnington. A moment later, the office door opened again, and Stephanie thrust a sheaf of papers towards Shadow.

"There you go—that's the lot," she said.

"Thank you for your help," Shadow started to reply, but she had slammed the door shut again before he could finish.

The two detectives and Dr Shepherd made their way back down the stairs where the two Roman soldiers, who were now holding fearsome-looking weapons, were posing for photographs with three giggling Chinese tourists.

"Are those two gentlemen museum guides?" Shadow asked Dr Shepherd.

"No, Chief Inspector, Glenn and Peter are our security team. Having them dress that way was one of Stephanie's marketing ideas. As you can see the visitors love to take a picture with them and in more clement weather, they often walk around the city handing out leaflets and pointing tourists in our direction. Raising our profile, I believe it's called. Stephanie can certainly be very inventive, Chief Inspector."

Shadow wondered whether she had meant to say innovative. Dr Shepherd didn't seem like a woman who confused her words, but before he could query this, he sensed Jimmy peering over his shoulder to read the list Stephanie had given him.

"Glenn Denton and Peter Spears. His name is Spears and look he's carrying one too now." Jimmy laughed. Shadow scowled and shifted the list out of Jimmy's view.

"Your powers of observation are as keen as ever, Sergeant," he muttered, then turned his attention back to Dr Shepherd. "Their costumes and weapons are accurate copies of what a Roman solider would have worn I take it, Dr Shepherd."

"Oh yes, absolutely. Quite expensive of course, but it was something I insisted upon."

Before she could say any more, Dunnington came striding towards them, rubbing his hands together.

"Ah there you are! How's it all going? Case cracked yet?" he asked.

Shadow frowned. Was he joking? They'd been at the museum less than an hour.

"These are just preliminary enquiries, Mr Dunnington. We will need to return, probably with our forensics team, and we will need to speak to all members of staff," he explained sounding more patient than he felt.

"Really, oh that is disappointing. I thought you'd have, I don't know, got out a magnifying glass, found a few fingerprints and job done. Oh well, I suppose if you need more time there's not a lot I can do about it, but try and keep it all low-key will you, Shadow? What is it they say, discretion's the better part of valour and all that?"

"We'll try our best, Mr Dunnington," replied Shadow through gritted teeth. "I've met your security team," he added nodding in the direction of the retreating Roman soldiers.

"Ah yes, Pete and Glenn, good chaps, both ex-army, totally reliable. Glenn is a Brummie, real salt-of-the-earth type, and Pete hails from Colchester coincidentally."

At that moment Stephanie barged past them on her way down the stairs.

"Stephanie darling, where are you going? There's a letter I was hoping you might be able to type for me," Dunnington called out. Stephanie paused and tossed her hair as she pouted back at him.

"Not now, Timmy!" She pointed and glared at Shadow. "Thanks to him I've had a really stressful morning. I'm going to pop out for a little while. I need some retail therapy."

"All right then, darling, I'll leave it on your desk, shall I? Unless you'd like me to come with you?" Dunnington called out after her, but she had already disappeared through the main entrance doors. Shadow could barely believe his ears. Dunnington had called them out to investigate a major theft, provided them with very little information and was now considering swanning off to go shopping with his wife.

"We'll be on our way too, Mr Dunnington, and continue with our enquiries back at the station. As I said, tomorrow I'd like our forensics team to take a look at the storeroom, if that's convenient."

"I suppose so. Do you think they could be in and out before we open?"

"We'll try our best," repeated Shadow as he too headed towards the door with Jimmy not far behind him.

Chapter Two

Across 1.
Good lip care ensures you won't look like a fake (7 letters)

WHEN THEY STEPPED out into Exhibition Square sleety rain was beginning to fall.

"What do you think, Chief?" asked Jimmy as soon as they were out of earshot. "It's weird nobody noticed all those coins had been switched isn't it? I bet Stather had something to do with it. My money's on him."

Shadow raised an eyebrow. Jimmy had a habit of making unintentional puns.

"Any particular reason for suspecting Dr Stather, Sergeant?"

"Well he's always been a bit dodgy. Remember all those lies he told us before about finding a tunnel in Museum Gardens."

"I think we might need a little more than that to accuse him of theft, Sergeant. Mr Dunnington certainly seems to value his opinion over Dr Shepherd's."

"Stather looked really shifty, and he was pretty quiet in Dunnington's office. Maybe he has a guilty conscience," persisted Jimmy.

"Or perhaps he was concerned we would mention his involvement in a murder investigation. I doubt he would want that affecting his standing on the eyes of Dr Shepherd or Dunnington."

The two detectives waited for the traffic lights to turn to red again before crossing the road. The sleet was turning to snow and they ducked beneath the arches of the Theatre Royal to shelter for a moment.

"Oh great, I hope it lays. York looks really pretty covered in snow," commented Jimmy happily, despite winding his scarf even more tightly around his neck and rifling through his pockets for a pair of woolly gloves.

"It won't. The ground's too wet," replied Shadow bluntly. At times like this he wondered at what age he'd started finding snow an inconvenience rather than magical and exciting. Whatever age it was his sergeant showed no sign of reaching it any time soon.

"Is it just me, Chief, or does Dunnington seem a bit, well, dim?" asked Jimmy, who was now blowing on to his gloved fingers and stamping his feet.

"Well I certainly don't think he's the sharpest knife in the drawer, Sergeant."

"Then how did he get to be director of a museum?"

"I imagine it was thanks to his name. The Dunningtons are one of the city's oldest families, and as Dr Shepherd told us they were one of the founders of the museum."

"That's a really rubbish reason to give someone a job," replied Jimmy. Shadow smiled to himself. It was unlike his sergeant to be negative about anyone, but on this occasion, he agreed with him wholeheartedly.

"What if Dunnington is only pretending to be thick? Maybe he could have done it to claim the insurance."

Shadow raised a sceptical eyebrow.

"Let me guess you've recently watched a film involving an elaborate insurance scam."

"Yeh, sort of, *The Thomas Crown Affair*. Have you seen it, Chief?"

Shadow shook his head. He never watched television or went to the cinema. Unfortunately both forms of entertainment heavily influenced his sergeant's theories.

"What did you make of Dr Shepherd?" he asked. "Didn't you find it strange that she still wore protective gloves to handle the coins even though she knew they were fakes?"

"No." Jimmy shook his head firmly. "I think she was just being extra careful. They were still pretty delicate, or maybe she did it out of habit. I thought she seemed nice and really interesting, especially when she was talking about St Valentine. There's no way she's involved. You know sometimes, Chief, you can be really suspicious."

"Yes, well that is sort of my job, Sergeant," replied Shadow tersely. Not for the first time, he thought his sergeant might have been better suited to social work. They were both silent for a moment as they watched the snowstorm stop as quickly as it had started.

"I've had an idea, Chief," Jimmy said, his voice sounding muffled beneath his scarf. "You'd need to be pretty skilled at working with gold to copy those coins. Maybe we should ask a jeweller their opinion. Do you remember, Ellie Treanor? We met her when she designed a Viking bracelet in the Alfred Campbell case. She's got a studio over on Swinegate. We could see what she thinks."

Shadow gave a wry smile as he slowly nodded.

"And she's also the lady you bought Sophie's birthday present from, therefore maybe while we're there you could look for yet more inspiration for Valentine's Day. You really are about as subtle as a brick, Sergeant."

"Well it wouldn't hurt to look would it, Chief?" replied Jimmy.

"Come on then," said Shadow with a sigh as he turned up the collar of his jacket. "I don't care where we go as long as it's warmer than here. Actually, come to think of it, didn't there used to be a shop down Swinegate that dealt in old coins and stamps?"

Shadow thrust his hands deep into the pockets of his jacket and the two detectives headed along the slush-covered pavement towards Petergate.

THE SWINEGATE QUARTER was situated off Petergate. It was

a tangle of medieval streets laying roughly in a square. It was also bordered by Stonegate, Church Street and St Sampson's Square. As well as Swinegate itself there was Grape Lane and Little Stonegate. For centuries the area had been the traditional haunt of the city's prostitutes, but more recently it had gone through a process of gentrification and was now home to fashionable cocktail bars, exclusive boutiques and artisans' studios. On the corner of Grape Lane, there was a shop selling handmade chocolates that happened to be Sophie's favourite. As the two detectives passed by the window, the pretty young woman behind the counter looked up. When she saw Jimmy, she waved and gave him a huge smile.

"Oh wow! I haven't seen Luce for ages. Is it okay if we call in here for a second, Chief?" Jimmy asked, pushing the door open before Shadow had a chance to respond. With a sigh of resignation, he followed his sergeant inside.

Luce's full name turned out to be Lucy Wang and she was clearly a close friend of his sergeant's. The young woman dashed from behind the counter and threw her arms around Jimmy's neck. Looking a little embarrassed, Jimmy introduced her to Shadow, who then discreetly stepped back. He strolled around the piles of chocolates displayed artistically as the two young people caught up with each other's news. It seemed Lucy had recently returned from a year in Taiwan. She was helping out in the chocolate shop, where she'd previously had a job as a student, because Valentine's was such a busy time for them. Shadow peered through the small window in the door to the kitchen and saw a slightly har-assed-looking man with a moustache spreading a thick layer of chocolate on to the marble worktop as two assistants carefully used tongs to place truffles into tissue-lined gift boxes.

"So, do you have any plans now that you're home?" he heard Jimmy ask.

"I'd really like to help out with Dad's business. I've got a couple of great ideas that I think could work, but you know what he's like. He doesn't handle change well," replied Lucy.

"He and my mum both." Jimmy laughed, then glancing over to Shadow. "Look, I'll have to go, but I'll catch you later okay, Luce."

Shadow nodded politely to the young woman as they left.

"What business does her father own?" he asked when they were outside.

"Mr Wang has a tea shop off Goodramgate, Chief. He imports and sells loose tea from China and there's a room where you are served tea in the traditional Chinese way. It's always been popular with tourists and the Chinese community here in York. My mum and her friends still go all the time, but I hear it might not be doing as well as it used to. It'll be good for him to have Lucy back to help out. Her mum died not long after I lost my dad. I guess that's why we've always been really close."

"Like having another sister?" suggested Shadow.

Jimmy shook his head. "No way, Angela is such a pain. Luce is much cooler. She's a great cook too. Hopefully, she'll make her fortune cookies for the New Year dinner. They aren't really traditional, but the English guests think they are fun, so Mum always serves them. You are still coming aren't you, Chief?"

Shadow made a noncommittal grunting noise in response. Rose had insisted he join them, but he really didn't enjoy parties. He would have to try and think of an excuse.

"Look, this used to be the coin shop," he said instead, pointing to the shop next to the chocolatier's. It looked like it had recently been painted, but it was now empty with only a 'to let' sign in the window. A little farther along the street was Ellie Treanor's Design Studio. They stepped inside the warm, subtly lit studio and the jewellery designer recognised them at once. Ellie Treanor was a large woman with a fondness for dressing in velvet smocks. Her long dark hair was piled up on her head as always with two pencils sticking out. Shadow was never sure if they were securing the hair or had just been placed there for safekeeping.

"How nice to see you again, Sergeant Chang, Chief Inspector Shadow. Should I be worried or is this a social visit?"

"Nothing to worry about, Miss Treanor," Shadow reassured her. "We just hoped you would be able to give your professional opinion on something."

Miss Treanor blushed, and her hands fluttered around her face self-consciously.

"Goodness me! I don't know if I'll be much use, Chief Inspector, but I'll certainly try my best to help you if I can."

"Thank you very much. Sergeant Chang has some photographs of various Roman coins and a ring we would like you to look at," Shadow explained, but when he turned to look for Jimmy, he found his sergeant was already distracted. He was peering into a cabinet holding various rings set with precious stones. Shadow cleared his throat loudly. Jimmy looked up.

"Yes, Chief?"

"The photographs when you have a moment please, Sergeant."

Jimmy gave an apologetic smile as he fished his phone out of his pocket and showed the screen to Miss Treanor.

"Do you ever produce replicas of coins like these, perhaps to be worn as a pendent?" asked Shadow, as Jimmy scrolled through the images.

"If only," replied Miss Treanor with a wistful sigh. "They are beautiful, but unfortunately it would simply be too time-consuming to be profitable."

"But there is a market for them?"

"I don't know about coins, but there definitely is for Roman-style jewellery. I believe the Russian and Chinese buyers are especially interested."

"And if I wanted to buy an original piece of Roman jewellery rather than a replica, where would you advise me to go?"

"I would probably contact one of the international auction houses down in London. They check the authenticity of each piece and, as I said, they are very popular with foreign buyers."

"Are there any other jewellery designers in the city?" Shadow asked. He didn't think the original museum pieces were likely to still be in the country let alone York, but he wondered if the copies could have been created close by. Surely whoever copied them would have needed time to study each piece. Perhaps they had visited the museum when the stolen pieces were on display.

"You could try speaking to Jacqui. She used to be my neighbour here but a few months ago she moved to one of those new units at Monk Bar Court."

"I thought the shop next to you used to be the coin shop," queried Shadow.

"Oh that was several years ago, Chief Inspector. Long before my time. Mr Level was the owner's name. I hear he was quite a character. Jacqui took over the shop when he died a couple of years ago, but it was empty for a while before then."

"Jacqui...?"

"Oh yes of course, Chief Inspector, a surname would help wouldn't it? Jacqui Heaton."

"Why did she move? Surely being here is more central?" asked Jimmy.

Ellie pursed her lips. "You'll have to ask Jacqui about

that. She obviously found something attractive about the place. Personally, I couldn't see the appeal."

THE TWO DETECTIVES left the Swinegate Quarter and headed past the Minster towards Monk Bar.

"You know, Chief, Ellie had a really pretty ring in her studio. It looked a lot like the Roman one Dr Shepherd showed us," began Jimmy, but Shadow held up his hand to halt him.

"Was it an exact replica and therefore a possible link to our investigation, Sergeant?"

"Er, no, Chief."

"Then I don't need to hear about it."

They turned down Goodramgate with Jimmy stopping briefly to buy a takeaway coffee on the way. Shadow watched in amusement as his shivering sergeant tightly gripped the cup of hot liquid in his freezing hands.

"Have you never thought of emigrating to a warmer country, Sergeant?" he asked.

"Oh I couldn't live anywhere else, Chief. I absolutely love it here. I just don't like the cold and the damp, or the wind and the rain."

"Well then fortunately for you that only describes North Yorkshire for about eleven months of the year," replied Shadow.

MONK BAR COURT was a narrow alleyway that ran alongside the city walls. It was next to Monk Bar, one of the gateways into the city. Shadow could remember when it had been called Elbow Lane and was known as one of the most rundown and dilapidated streets in York. Like the Swinegate Quarter it had recently been gentrified and the row of broken-down cottages were being renovated with a view to accommodating artisans.

Mr Wang's tea shop stood on the corner at the entrance to Monk Bar Court. Unlike the businesses opening behind him, his shop had been a feature of the street for over twenty years. The owner was outside sweeping the remaining slush from the pavement in front of his door.

"Good morning, Mr Wang. How are you?" asked Jimmy politely.

"I am well, but business could be better," replied the older man bluntly. "I blame the younger generation and their obsession with coffee," he said pointedly glaring at the paper cup in Jimmy's hand. Jimmy turned red with embarrassment.

"I've just seen Lucy. You must be pleased she's home."

Mr Wang waved his hand dismissively. "Lucy is a good girl, but she wants to change everything. Sometimes the old ways are the best."

With that he turned and went back inside his empty

shop and the two detectives carried on through the archway to the new shops. 'Chocolates from Old Elbow Lane' stood next to 'Monk Court Jewellery'. The third and fourth units at the end of the row looked like they were still being renovated, with a builder's van and a cement mixer standing outside.

Shadow and Jimmy stepped into the jewellery boutique. Like Ellie Treanor's place it was small and carefully lit with white walls, polished wood floor and glass cabinets displaying various items of jewellery. Jazz music was playing in the background, although it was so loud, the lady sitting behind the counter didn't hear them come in.

"Miss Heaton?" enquired Shadow raising his own voice above that of Fred Astaire's singing about his 'Top Hat, White Tie, and Tails'. The lady behind the counter stood up and smiled.

"Yes, can I help you, gentlemen?" she asked. Shadow introduced himself and Jimmy.

Jacqui Heaton was a thin, angular woman with a sharply cut geometric black bob. Like Ellie Treanor she dressed a little eccentrically. As she came to greet them, Shadow could see she was wearing black lace fingerless gloves, a white high-necked frilly blouse beneath a purple crushed velvet suit with a skirt that reached down to her ankles. Peeping out below that skirt were a pair of crimson high-heeled court shoes.

"We were wondering if we could ask you some questions about Roman jewellery?" he said.

"Ask away, Chief Inspector, but it's not really my thing. I'm strictly an art deco girl."

Shadow's eyes briefly scanned the room and took in the geometric designs of the silver jewellery on display and the posters adorning the walls from the 1920s and 30s.

"So I see, Miss Heaton. You are also a jazz fan," he replied, struggling to make himself heard above Marlene Dietrich who had now taken the place of Fred.

"Absolutely, sorry if it's a bit loud. Paul rigged up the sound system for me, but the volume keeps sticking."

"Paul?" enquired Shadow. He was a huge jazz fan himself, but how on earth did Jacqui ever manage to converse with her customers?

"Paul Le Vel. He has the chocolatier's next door. We moved here together," she explained and Shadow noticed she blushed a little as she spoke about her neighbour, then as if reading his mind: "Fortunately, most of my customers are online at this time of year."

"Would it be possible to speak upstairs instead?" he asked.

"Sorry, I don't have the keys. There's a flat above here, but I can't move in for another six months, when the lease on my current place runs out. Paul's trying to sublet it for me until then. He lives above his shop you see. That means he's always here to let any prospective tenants view it. He's such a star. I don't know what I'd do without him. I've got a workshop in the back, but it's just as noisy in there."

Shadow nodded and tried to press on.

"So, nobody has approached you to design any Roman jewellery or coins for them?" he asked. Jacqui shook her head and was about to answer when the door swung open and a tall, good-looking, blond man strode in and planted a kiss on Jacqui's cheek.

"Hello, gorgeous girl! How's my favourite jeweller? Honestly, I turn my back for two minutes and other men are trying to chat you up."

He turned and winked at the two detectives as Jacqui blushed and giggled.

"Oh, Paul, don't be silly! This is Chief Inspector Shadow and Sergeant Chang," she told him.

Paul held up his hands in a dramatic gesture of surrender. "It's all right, officers, I'll come quietly," he said with a grin.

Shadow remained stony-faced. He couldn't recall ever taking such an instant dislike to someone as he had to the irritating man in front of him, who was now holding out his hand.

"Paul Le Vel, local businessman and general nuisance, isn't that right, Jacs?"

"Oh, Paul, you are funny!" gushed Jacqui as Jimmy shook Le Vel's hand and Shadow reluctantly did the same.

"Why don't you come next door where it's quieter and I'll even throw in a couple of our handmade chocolates— exactly what you need to go with that coffee, Sergeant," Le

Vel suggested.

"That would be great, thanks very much," replied Jimmy before Shadow had a chance to decline the offer.

"Always happy to help the boys in blue; besides you can't hear yourself think in here. I promise to fix the volume soon, Jacs darling," he called over his shoulder as he headed out the door followed by Jimmy and Shadow, who had begun grinding his teeth. Jacqui stuck a back in five minutes sign on the door before locking up and joining them too.

Parked on the cobbles outside the shops were two vehicles. A vintage delivery van painted brown and bearing the name 'Chocolates from Old Elbow Lane' and a bright red MG sports car with the registration 100 LEV that Shadow assumed belonged to Le Vel. With Jimmy there, he didn't need to assume for long.

"That's a beautiful car you have, Mr Le Vel," remarked his sergeant.

"Yes, it's a nifty little number and very popular with the ladies—a bit like her owner." Le Vel laughed.

They followed Le Vel through the door of his own shop that was fitted with a shiny brass jangling bell. The interior was styled to look like a Victorian chocolatier's with dark wood floors and cabinets, an old-fashioned cash register, marble countertop and brass weighing scales. Vases of red roses were tastefully arranged here and there along with neatly stacked dark red gift boxes. The elaborate gold writing on the boxes gave the name of the shop and declared that the chocolates inside were sent with love. Shadow doubted the recipients would be quite so keen to eat the contents if they knew that Elbow Lane had once been the site of the city's midden. He guessed this fact wasn't something Paul Le Vel would be using to promote his business.

"Hello, my lovelies, how are we all?" Le Vel called out to four teenage girls, who were wearing Victorian-style black dresses with frilly white aprons and white mop caps. Two were standing behind the counter and two could be seen through the open door into the kitchen, their faces covered by protective masks as they decorated a tray of chocolates with red and white icing.

"We were just asking Miss Heaton if she ever designed Roman jewellery," Jimmy started to explain.

"But I told them I'm strictly art deco," said Jacqui.

"And all that jazz," sang Le Vel while shimmying and doing jazz hands, before directing his attention to Jimmy. "Now, Sergeant, what can I tempt you with? A soft centre, something nutty, a cheeky caramel maybe?"

While Le Vel fussed around offering Jimmy various flavours to try, Shadow had a chance to study their host. He guessed he was about forty years old, but he dressed like a much younger man. His shirt was untucked over his designer jeans and expensive trainers that Shadow was more used to seeing adorn his sergeant's feet. He was wearing a waistcoat and an elaborately knotted silk scarf around his neck. Le Vel wore his hair in a floppy boyish style and the chief inspector strongly suspected its blond tones were chemically enhanced. Grudgingly Shadow had to admit that with his blue eyes, high cheekbones and ready smile he could be called handsome. Judging by the blushes and shy smiles, his workforce and his neighbour certainly seemed to think so.

Shadow's nose twitched. York had a long history of making chocolate. His own mother had worked in one of the many factories after his father died. When the wind was blowing in the right direction, the sweet rich smell from the factories drifted across the city. Yet, in here there was barely any scent of chocolate at all.

"How's business, Mr Le Vel?" he asked.

"I mustn't grumble, Chief Inspector," Le Vel said with another easy smile.

"Competition must be fierce in a city with so many other chocolatiers."

"It's all about the marketing," replied Le Vel. Shadow raised an eyebrow but didn't say anything. He had thought if you were selling handmade chocolates it would be all about the taste.

"Do you make the chocolates yourself?"

"They're all made to my specifications," he replied smoothly, "but these lovely girls are far better at finishing the decorative details than me. Smaller hands you see." He briefly paused and lifted the hand of one of his assistants and brushed it with his lips. The girl giggled and Shadow wondered if Le Vel had ever heard of the rules governing sexual harassment in the workplace.

"Paul does really well in the export market. He sells loads to Europe and the Far East," gushed Jacqui. Shadow looked at Le Vel enquiringly, who raised his hands in mock embarrassment.

"I'll never need to pay for advertising with Jac's around will I, darling, but yes I have been very lucky with some of my international customers."

"You are too modest, Paul! And look at these lovely shoes he bought me last time he went to China," Jacqui continued, raising her skirt to show off her red shoes.

"I know how you struggle over here with your tiny feet, darling. She has pretty little dancer's feet, gentlemen."

Jacqui's face flushed with pleasure, and she looked self-conscious.

"Well if I do, they make up for my ugly old hands." She peeled back about an inch of her lace gloves to reveal several vivid red scars. "I was a little careless with the soldering iron when I was doing my training."

Paul reached across, took her hand and placed a kiss on the scars.

"They are the hands of an artist," he declared.

"Oh, Paul, you do say the sweetest things," she simpered.

Shadow was beginning to feel quite queasy and it wasn't from being surrounded by chocolate.

At that moment Jimmy's phone rang loudly from inside his pocket. With an apologetic look, he swallowed down his mouthful of caramel and ducked outside to answer it. It was with some relief that Shadow took this as his cue to say goodbye to Jacqui and Le Vel. He couldn't see either of them being much use in helping him locate the missing coins. As he left the chocolate shop, Lucy Wang was arriving, her arms full of boxes. Shadow held the door as she carefully reversed in.

"Ah luscious Lucy here to save the day," he heard Le Vel call out. With her back to the shop, Lucy looked Shadow in the eye and stuck her tongue out as if she were being sick. Shadow gave a small smile. It seemed that at least one female was immune to Le Vel's charms.

"That was the station, Chief," said Jimmy as he slipped his phone back into his pocket. "The receptionist from the Monk Bar Hotel called to say he thinks a member of a tour party staying there has disappeared."

"Thinks?"

"Well it seems the tourist is a young Chinese woman. That's why Tom called me. The receptionist was a bit flustered, but he thinks that's what some of the other members of the tour party were trying to tell him."

"I suppose we should pay them a visit then," said Shadow with a sigh. "Between the museum director who doesn't realise he's been burgled and a girl that may or may not be missing, we are getting nowhere fast today. Didn't you think it was strange that Le Vel never asked us why we were at Jacqui's place before inviting us to his shop? Most people are concerned when they hear who we are. They automatically think we're the bearers of bad news."

"Well I guess we are usually, but maybe he didn't want to be nosy. I just don't think you liked him very much, Chief. You never stopped scowling all the time you were in there."

"Don't exaggerate, Sergeant, I was perfectly polite, but I did think he was a bit over the top, didn't you?"

"He seemed okay," replied Jimmy with a shrug, "and his chocolates tasted just as good as the one's from Swinegate."

THE MONK BAR Hotel was situated outside the city walls and less than a two-minute walk away. It was a smart modern hotel popular with touring coach parties due to its large car park and proximity to the city centre. When the two detectives entered the lobby, they immediately saw the reception desk was surrounded by half a dozen very animated Chinese tourists. Shadow manoeuvred his way to the front and introduced himself and Jimmy to the flustered receptionist.

"Oh thank goodness you're here," said the red-faced young man. "They are ever so upset, but I can't understand what they're saying. I only got a D in GCSE French and that's not much help at all."

"No it wouldn't be," agreed Shadow. "Don't they have a

tour guide to act as a translator?"

"Yes, but he's not answering his mobile, sir."

Shadow turned to Jimmy, only to find the tourists had already surrounded him and were all talking to him at the same time. His sergeant was trying, not very successfully, to calm them down and make himself heard above the noise. After a few moments, he attempted to translate back to Shadow.

"They all arrived on the coach yesterday morning, but nobody has seen the girl since they were all in the Museum Gardens at about 10.30am. That's over twenty-four hours ago now."

"Was this girl travelling alone?"

"Yes, I think so."

"Why are they all so angry?" asked Shadow, loud enough to briefly silence the group, who turned round to stare at him.

"They aren't really, Chief. It's just the way the Beijing accent sounds sometimes; you know the different tones they use."

Suddenly the whole group started talking again. An older lady wearing a yellow raincoat and large glasses began poking Jimmy in the chest.

"What now?" asked Shadow in exasperation.

"I asked them about the tour guide. They said he thinks the young woman could simply have gone to visit relatives, but this lady has just said the tour guide is an idiot and called him various rude names. That's when the others joined in. Apparently, he isn't living up to their expectations."

"Well then, I think I'll leave you to it. If you ever discover if this really is a case of a missing person, I'll be in the Royal Oak."

CHAPTER THREE

Down 2.
*Gertrude, Imogen, Nancy and Laura are initially not as popular
as the girl from Shanghai (4 letters)*

SHADOW LEFT THE chaos of the hotel reception behind
and headed back under Monk Bar and down Goodramgate to the Royal Oak. The pub had stood there since the
seventeenth century and even at this time of year was
festooned with colourful hanging baskets. He carefully
walked through the door and down the steps that he had
seen trip up more drunks than he cared to remember. At the
bar he ordered a pint of Black Sheep and the bacon chops
with fried eggs and chips. Then he took a seat on the leather
bench that ran along the wall beneath the window.

He took a sip of beer and turned his head. The window
looked out on to Goodramgate and was directly opposite the
laundry Shadow used. It was run by Maggie, his old school
friend. He could see her quite clearly standing behind the
counter. It looked like she was regaling her two young
assistants, Karen and Ros, with some story or other. They
were laughing as she waved her arms around and pulled a

series of dramatic expressions. Shadow wished he could lip-read. Then he noticed Paul Le Vel walking towards Maggie's place carrying a tray of his chocolates aloft in one hand as if he was a waiter at The Savoy. He paused at the window, blowing exaggerated kisses to the three women inside, before pushing the door open.

Unfortunately, at that moment a brewery lorry pulled up outside, blocking his view. He frowned and took another sip of his pint before turning his attention to the information Stephanie had reluctantly provided him with. He removed the papers from his jacket pocket, unfolded them and spread them out on to the table.

THE FLOOR PLAN seemed quite straightforward. As he had guessed the museum's café was located directly beneath the storeroom, staff room and Stephanie's office. Next, he ran his eye down the staff list, noting that many of the names had the word 'volunteer' next to them. Apart from the two security guards and Stephanie herself most of the staff, employed or otherwise, had been there for years. Dr Shepherd had been there almost three years. Beneath the details of the staff, there was also a list of the Board of Trustees. There were five in total. Dunnington's name was there, as was Stather's and two other names Shadow recognised. Cornelius Rutherford, one of the most well-respected solicitors in the city and Jonty Woodhead, who owned a firm of accountants. The fifth name was a history professor at the university. Shadow had always found Rutherford to be helpful and decided to call the solicitor when he returned to the office.

At that moment, his lunch arrived. He quickly cleared away the papers and for a little while he forgot all about Roman coins and missing girls. He'd just finished the last mouthful and was leaning back with a satisfied sigh when Jimmy arrived, looking a little flustered.

"Sorry, I've been a while, Chief, it was quite difficult to get away from Mrs Chen and all the others."

"Mrs Chen?"

"The lady wearing the large glasses and yellow coat. She was the one who insisted the hotel rang us."

"So is the girl missing or not?"

"Yes, at least I think so—" Jimmy turned on his electronic notebook "—but it all seems a bit weird. You see, the rest of the tour party are all from Beijing. They all left China together on the same plane and got on the coach at the airport—Heathrow. They had a few days in London before heading north. At about six o'clock yesterday morning they all left their hotel outside London, but the missing girl only joined them yesterday morning at one of the motorway service stations on the M1. Mrs Chen said she didn't speak much English, was very quiet and from Shanghai."

"Is that important?"

"The rest of the tour found it a bit strange. I guess it

would be like someone from Glasgow suddenly joining a group of Londoners. Mrs Chen also said she had the face of a pretty young girl, but the hands of an ugly old woman."

"What's that supposed to mean?" asked Shadow impatiently, but Jimmy only shrugged. "Do we at least have a name?"

"Yes, Ling Li."

"Well that's something. Ling Li from Shanghai. You can go on that internet you are so fond of and start searching."

Jimmy groaned.

"What's wrong?" asked Shadow. "I thought you'd be pleased. Spending the afternoon in a nice warm office messing about on your computer."

"It's just that Ling Li is a really popular name, Chief. Like Sarah Smith would be over here and there must be almost thirty million people in Shanghai."

Shadow finished the last of his pint and stood up.

"Then we should probably make a move, Sergeant."

WHEN THEY RETURNED to the station, Shadow's first call was to Cornelius Rutherford.

"Oh no, who's died now?" was the solicitor's greeting when he heard Shadow's voice.

"Nobody as far as I know," replied Shadow. "I wanted to speak to you about the Eboracum Museum. I understand you are on the board."

"Yes, for my sins. Is this about the theft? I'm pleased Dunnington has finally seen sense and called you in. For a moment, I actually think he believed he wouldn't need to report it and could pretend the fakes are genuine."

"Really?" asked Shadow incredulously.

"You may have noticed logic isn't his strong point. We were at school together you know. He was a total duffer! But, well there has always been a Dunnington on the board of the Eboracum. Come to think of it I'm probably only there because a Rutherford was on the first board—another Cornelius. Jonty Woodhead is the same," he continued referring to the head of York's largest accountancy firm and a member of another of the city's oldest families. "Actually, I tried to step down last year, but Tim and Jonty talked me out of it."

"Why did you want to leave?"

"Well I was acting for Camilla, Tim's first wife, during their divorce and I thought it might make things a tad awkward."

"What happened with the divorce?"

"It was amicable enough in the end, I suppose. Camilla is a real stalwart. They'd been married for twenty-odd years and she practically ran the museum. She was a colonel's daughter and had worked for the National Trust. Organising the place was second nature to her. There were never any problems when Camilla was in charge, but her mother had a stroke a few years ago, so she went home to Suffolk to help take care of her as often as she could. As her mother's condition didn't improve, she spent more time there, months sometimes, and the temping agency sent Stephanie to help out and, well, the rest is history as they say."

"What about Dr Dorothy Shepherd? How would you describe her relationship with Dunnington?"

"A bit sticky. He really wanted Stather as curator, but Stather didn't want to give up his post at the Historic Foundation. The board didn't think he could do both roles, so the job was given to Dorothy. Naturally it doesn't help that she's a Quaker and Dunnington is ex-army."

"Dunnington was a soldier?" asked Shadow in surprise. Dunnington didn't strike him as the sort of man who could fight his way out of a paper bag let alone defend the realm.

"Yes a family tradition. His father was a major. Tim got through Sandhurst by the skin of his teeth but didn't last much longer. His family didn't know what else to do with him; therefore he ended up at the museum. Just another family tradition I suppose."

SHADOW SPENT THE next hour telephoning various London auction houses. Each coin expert he spoke to with their cut-glass accents and double-barrelled surnames told him the same thing. No Roman coins of the quantity and quality he was describing had been seen on the open market for years and if they were to come up for auction, they would attract a great deal of interest. As he put down the telephone for the fifth time, there was a cheerful rat-a-tat-tat on the door.

"Yes, Jimmy," called out Shadow. Sure enough the door opened and his sergeant stepped into the office. "Anything?"

"Not much, Chief. Shanghai is seven hours ahead of us, so most offices are closed, but I did finally speak to the tour guide. This is his first tour with the company. He wasn't expecting Ling to join yesterday morning, but she told him she had missed her flight and had rushed to catch them up. Apparently, she'd hitched her way to the service station in a van. She had a ticket for the tour that looked genuine, so he let her join. I also checked with the night manager at the hotel and Ling definitely didn't check in yesterday."

Shadow frowned.

"If she didn't speak much English, how on earth did she manage to tell a van driver to take her to a service station and, for that matter, how would she know where the coach would stop?"

"I don't know, Chief," replied Jimmy, "but anyway, as I wasn't getting very far in the search for information about Ling Li, I googled Roman coins and some of them are really valuable. A couple of years ago, one found by a metal detectorist in Kent sold at auction for $700,000 to a private collector."

"Yes, the auction houses told me something similar. I

suppose at least we have a definite motive for the theft. All we need now is the time, the culprit and some evidence." Shadow sighed. Jimmy's phone started bleeping and he groaned.

"What's wrong?"

"It's Mrs Chen. She keeps texting me to see if I have found Ling yet." His phone bleeped again several times. "Now she's got the whole tour party involved. They are all sending me photos and videos. Maybe it wasn't such a good idea to give them my mobile number."

"Let me see," said Shadow.

"Ling is the girl in the pink sweatshirt," said Jimmy turning the screen of his phone towards him. Shadow put his glasses on and squinted. The photo had been taken in Museum Gardens. It showed several of the group in front of the Hospitium. Shadow studied the missing girl's face, trying to read her expression. Her smile seemed a little nervous. She certainly didn't look like a carefree tourist enjoying her holiday.

"Mrs Chen said Ling disappeared not long after this photo was taken. What do you think, Chief, could she have been abducted or did she get separated from the group and now she's lost? Maybe she doesn't speak English, but if someone came across her and she was upset, then they would probably have contacted us," Jimmy wondered aloud.

Shadow stood up as his sergeant's phone pinged and bleeped. The sleety rain was battering his window again as he looked down on the swollen River Ouse. The brown, churning water was flowing rapidly towards Lendal Bridge. Living on *Florence*, his narrow boat all these years, Shadow was more aware than most of the power of the river.

"We could be making this too complicated," he said almost to himself.

"What do you mean, Chief?" asked Jimmy, briefly looking up from his constant stream of messages.

"Perhaps there isn't anything sinister about Ling's disappearance. Maybe nobody else was involved. Maybe she wandered away from the group, got too close to the river trying to take a photo or something and fell in."

"Surely someone would have seen or heard something," replied Jimmy. Shadow pulled on his coat.

"Not necessarily. It was only mid-morning and the Museum Gardens are often quiet at this time of year. I'm going down there to take a look. You call out the dive team and tell them to meet me there. Get that photo of her in the press too. It's about time MacNab actually did something useful," he ordered referring to a journalist on the local paper—*The Herald*—and one of his least favourite people. "Just say we're interested in her whereabouts and concerned for her safety. Ask her or anyone who has seen her to get in touch."

"It hasn't been forty-eight hours yet, Chief," protested Jimmy.

"I know, I know, but the current is strong right now. If she is down there we've got to try and find her sooner rather than later," replied Shadow as he headed out the door.

THE LEADEN SKY was growing steadily darker as the police divers surfaced for the fourth time. Once again they shook their heads. Shadow watched silently from the path by the river in Museum Gardens. He'd been standing there for over two hours and in all that time had barely seen another soul except for the divers. Jimmy had brought him a welcome takeaway coffee about an hour ago but had only stayed briefly as he was waiting to hear back from the Chinese embassy in London and the tour company's head office.

Shadow looked at his watch then signalled to the dive team to call it a day. There wasn't enough light for another attempt and the divers had already confirmed his fear that the current was so strong that if she had fallen in, there was a good chance she had been carried much farther downstream. No doubt in the morning he could expect a call from the chief constable, haranguing him for wasting resources. Shadow watched as the dive team's boat headed away down the river, then he turned and began to walk back through the gardens. As he did so, a faint orange glow from beneath Lendal Bridge caught his eyes. He walked towards it, pausing to pick up a couple of dry twigs and sticks along the way.

As usual, Missy greeted his arrival by barking loudly and aggressively and as usual Shadow ignored the irate spaniel.

He threw the wood on the fire in the small brazier. Jake, an ex-soldier, was sitting cross-legged on a folded-up sleeping bag. A rucksack rested against the wall next to him. He was dressed in combat trousers and a heavy camouflage jacket. When he saw Shadow, he briefly looked up from the sketch he'd been drawing on the flyleaf of an old Colin Dexter paperback. He and Missy had been living on the streets of York for several years, but Shadow hadn't seen the two of them for a while.

"You've been away," he said, more as a statement than a question.

"You know me and Missy, Mr Shadow—we prefer to winter in the Caribbean."

A smile flickered across Shadow's face as he held his hands towards the warmth of the flames. Jake put down his pencil and removed a cigarette from behind his ear, leant forward and lit it from the fire.

"We thought we'd try our luck down in London," he explained as he took a long drag. "Whoever said the streets there are paved with gold needs their eyes testing. I saw the dive team was out. You looking for another dead girl?"

"Maybe," replied Shadow. The last time their paths had crossed, Shadow had been investigating the death of a girl whose body had been found in the Museum Gardens. "I heard they wanted to give you a medal for helping Sergeant Chang that day."

Jake gave Shadow a wry smile.

"I told them to shove it. I've got more medals than the Prince of Wales, for all the good they've done me." He raised the cigarette to his lips again. "You know I've always found the river a peaceful place. Doesn't seem that way for everyone. Did you find her?"

"No." Shadow sighed. "I don't suppose you saw her? She was here yesterday morning, a Chinese girl in her late teens, early twenties maybe."

"Are you having a laugh? Every other person who walks through these gardens is a Chinese tourist."

Shadow put his hand in his pocket and took out the photo from Mrs Chen that Jimmy had enlarged and printed off for him. He unfolded it and showed it to Jake.

"That girl in particular. The one in the pink top."

Jake gave the photo a brief glance then nodded. "Yeh, as it happens, I did see her."

"You sound very sure all of a sudden."

"On the back of that pink top was a big picture of a cartoon dog. I saw it and thought it looked like Missy, here." He gave the spaniel who was now curled up next to him an affectionate pat.

"Where was she when you saw her?"

"Over by the abbey ruins," he said pointing to the far corner of the gardens where the remains of St Mary's Abbey stood.

"Was she on her own?"

"When I saw her, she was talking to that Rupert who

runs the Roman Museum. It looked like she was asking for directions or something."

Shadow frowned. Why was Dunnington talking to Ling? Was it just a coincidence? He didn't know, but he did know that Rupert was a derogatory term for an officer in the British Army. It was used for someone who totally lacked any skill or common sense and had only obtained his rank through family connections. Rutherford had mentioned Tim Dunnington had briefly been in the army.

"Dunnington? Did you ever serve under him?" he asked.

Jake gave a firm shake of his head. "No thank God. He was as much use as a chocolate teapot. They kept moving him around. Colchester, Catterick, Aldershot—all the glamorous locations. He was a disaster wherever he went."

"Did he ever serve abroad?"

"Doubt it. He was a total liability. He'd have been a danger to his men."

Shadow nodded and remembered the other two ex-soldiers at the museum.

"What about Pete and Glenn, the two security guards at the museum? Did your paths ever cross?"

Jake raised the cigarette to his lips and inhaled deeply before replying.

"Don't know that guy Pete, but I remember Glenn. He was in logistics. Glenn the geisha we used to call him."

"Any particular reason?" Shadow asked, knowing the soldiers' sense of humour could be difficult to decipher to say the least.

Jake shrugged. "For a big bloke he's got really small feet."

SHADOW LEFT JAKE and Missy by their fire. He glanced at his watch. There was still a little time before they closed the garden gates. He walked over to the ruins of St Mary's Abbey. It had once been the wealthiest abbey in the North of England, but now all that was left were the crumbling remains of the north and west walls. North Yorkshire was littered with similar sites: Fountains, Rievaulx, Byland, Kirkham. They were the still-visible remains of Henry VIII's split with Rome. All because a power-crazed king wanted the pope to let him have a new wife, Shadow thought to himself.

Behind the ruins stood the half-timbered Abbot's House, now known as King's Manor and the Eboracum Museum. When he'd stood at the window in the museum he'd had a good view of the gardens, but down here on the ground most of the building was obscured by the ruins and in summer when the trees were in leaf it would be almost invisible.

He left the gardens and walked towards Petergate, still thinking about Dunnington. According to Cornelius Rutherford, he'd discarded a loyal wife of twenty years for a new, younger one, just like King Henry. Over the space of five hundred years it seemed human nature hadn't changed much at all.

THAT EVENING, LIKE almost every evening, Shadow made his way to one of the city's many Italian restaurants. Tonight, it was Catania on Goodramgate's turn. A waiter showed him to his usual table. As Shadow tried to remove his jacket, he became entangled in the red paper hearts dangling from the ceiling. Maria, the owner's wife, rushed over to assist him. She looked flushed and excited.

"Not long now until Valentine's! My favourite night of the year! So many couples. All young and in love. Last year we had a proposal in here. It was very romantic. I am hoping the same might happen this year. Gino has champagne chilling just in case! Then we can make a big party!"

Shadow glanced around suspiciously and silently prayed none of his fellow diners were feeling too romantically inclined this evening. If his empty stomach wasn't growling so loudly, he would have been tempted to ask for a takeaway. Instead he took his seat in the window and ordered a bottle of Chianti Classico, some focaccia and the medaglioni di manzo.

Although it was dark outside, thanks to the street lights Shadow had a front-row seat to the activities taking place out on Goodramgate. Despite the cold weather there were plenty of people enjoying the evening. Couples hurried by arm in arm and as usual large groups of tourists were stopping to photograph the Minster's magnificent East Window. Shadow watched as the Chinese party from the Monk Bar Hotel were herded past by a harassed-looking young tour guide wearing a baseball cap. It was impossible for him to know what was being said, but it seemed from her exaggerated hand gestures, Mrs Chen was berating him about something.

When they had gone, he spotted Dr Shepherd, with her long plait blowing in the wind, striding by on the other side of the road. She was heading in the opposite direction, towards the city walls. Shadow wondered where she was going, but at that moment his food arrived, and all thoughts of coins and missing tourists were pushed to one side.

He ate quickly, not only because he was hungry and the food was delicious, but also because he was eager to avoid any pre-Valentine's excitement. It seemed the candlelit tables surrounding him were full of couples gazing adoringly into each other's eyes. He paid his bill, pulled on his jacket and was about to head to the door, when a thought occurred to him.

"Gino, can I get a pizza to take away please?"

"You are still hungry?" his host asked, looking horrified that one of his best customers was leaving his restaurant less than satisfied.

"No, it's not for me," replied Shadow.

A few minutes later, with a boxed-up margarita pizza zipped into a thermal bag in his hands, he headed back to the steps by the side of Lendal Bridge. The brazier was still glowing orange as Jake and Missy sat curled up together beneath a sleeping bag. Shadow handed the pizza over without a word and carried on along the path by the river towards *Florence*.

"Missy prefers pepperoni," Jake shouted after him.

"Duly noted," Shadow shouted back.

THE NEXT MORNING after another satisfying breakfast at Bettys, Shadow headed to the station to collect Jimmy before returning to the Eboracum Museum. However, no sooner had he stepped through the door than he was informed by Tom, one of the young uniformed constables, that Jimmy had rushed out on an errand and asked if he could meet him outside the Minster instead. They had arranged to visit the Eboracum Museum again, this time with the forensics team. Shadow supposed the Minster was on his way, yet it still struck him as unusual behaviour from his sergeant.

Shadow strolled across the Minster plaza. It was a cold but bright morning. Tourists were sitting on the steps leading up to the door of the south transept, enjoying the winter sun. He waved to Angela, Jimmy's sister. She was a teacher and was shepherding young choristers in their bright red blazers back to the Minster School after their singing practice. There was no sign of Jimmy, however.

Shadow waited by the statue of Constantine the Great whose coins they had been studying the previous day.

Someone, probably a drunk student, had wrapped a university scarf around the neck of the man who had been declared Roman Emperor while he was here in York. He had converted to Christianity on his deathbed, an event that forever linked Rome to the church. Shadow looked up at the stone figure.

"You've got a lot to answer for," he muttered.

"They do say talking to yourself is the first sign of madness," said a familiar voice behind him. He spun around to find Maggie standing there. She was wearing a green wool coat and matching hat.

"I was talking to the statue," he said defensively.

"Oh well that's okay then," she replied with a grin. "That's perfectly normal."

"Well it's my only chance of a decent conversation these days. Anyway, what are you doing still here? I thought you usually disappeared off to sunny Spain this time of year."

"It's good to see you too, John," replied Maggie a note of sarcasm in her voice. "I decided to stay put this year and have my kitchen extended. I've been wanting to do it for ages and when the builders finally gave me a date, I didn't want to put them off. Now of course I'm regretting it. The ground is so wet their machinery is churning up the grass and making such a mess of my garden."

"Did I see Paul Le Vel at the laundry yesterday?" Shadow asked abruptly. There was something about the chocolatier that was still bothering him.

Maggie shrugged. "Probably—he's always popping in, trying to chat up Karen or Ros. Why do you ask? What's he been up to?"

"Nothing. Why do you think he'd have been up to something? Do you think he's dodgy?"

"Not really, but he's a charmer isn't he—a bit of a rogue with the gift of the gab, just like his father was."

"Who was his father?"

"Ernest Level, who used to have that shop on Swinegate buying and selling old coins and stamps. Don't you remember? He was a real charmer too, far too old for me of course, but he certainly liked the ladies and they seemed to like him too. There were a few broken hearts in the city the day he left."

As was often the case, Shadow was struggling to keep up with Maggie as she rattled away.

"Hold on, you're saying Paul Le Vel is really Paul Level. Why the name change?"

"I don't know, to make people think he's French I suppose. I heard him spinning Karen a yarn about how his noble ancestors bravely escaped the Revolution. I put her straight of course, but you've got to admit it sounds more glamorous," said Maggie.

"Pretentious more like," grunted Shadow. "Does he have any brothers or sisters?"

"Yes and no," began Maggie. "Paul's mother was Ernie's assistant and he married her. Paul's the only legitimate son, but let's just say Ernie wasn't the faithful type. He was always going off on business trips to Birmingham's jewellery quarter or down to Hatton Garden, not to mention abroad. While he was away, he wasn't only handling coins and stamps, if you catch my drift. At the final count, I think there were about half a dozen little Ernies in various corners of the world. Eventually, his wife got fed up and left him, but Paul stayed with his father. A few years ago, they left York and ended up in Hong Kong. Poor old Ernie died out there." She paused for a moment and frowned. "I forget what from."

"Exhaustion by the sound of things," replied Shadow. Maggie threw her head back and laughed.

"You might be right, John. Oh speak of the devil!"

Shadow turned to see Paul Le Vel sauntering across the plaza towards them. He was holding a large bunch of red roses and there was an even larger grin on his face.

"Margaret my darling," he declared withdrawing a single stem from the bunch and, with a theatrical bow, presented it to Maggie. "A rose for a rose."

"Thanks," she said, taking it with a bemused smile. Shadow noticed Le Vel had particularly large, pudgy fingers. They were like a bunch of bananas.

Paul turned his attention to Shadow. "Morning, Chief Inspector, you don't mind me interrupting you and the beautiful Margaret, do you?"

"Not at all—we were just chatting," replied Shadow through gritted teeth as Maggie raised the flower to her nose.

Why did the idiot keep calling her Margaret? Anyone who knew her, knew her real name was Magdalena.

"Then may I escort you to your empire, my lady?" He bowed again and, taking Maggie's arm, guiding her towards Goodramgate and breaking into the opening verse of 'Maggie May' as he did so. Maggie turned back briefly.

"Bye John," she called with a wave. Shadow raised his hand in response and watched the two of them go.

"What's up, Chief? You've got a face like thunder," asked Jimmy, whom he hadn't noticed arriving behind him. Shadow turned around in surprise, unaware he had been scowling.

"Where have you been?" he asked grumpily as he strode towards the Eboracum museum. Jimmy fell into step beside him.

"There was just something important I needed to do," he replied. Shadow thought his sergeant sound unusually evasive, but Le Vel was still on his mind.

"Why does he have so much spare time on his hands anyway?"

"Chief?"

"Paul Le Vel or Level. Whatever his name is. Why isn't he busy making chocolate instead of swanning around the city? Isn't Valentine's a busy time for him?"

"Yes, but he doesn't make the chocolates himself. He buys them wholesale from the guy on Swinegate and then gets the girls in the back to ice on his shop's motif. I told you they tasted just as good."

"That can't be very cost-effective," said Shadow, thinking how it also explained the lack of a chocolate aroma in Le Vel's kitchen. "How do you know all this anyway?"

"Lucy was telling me earlier."

"Was that your important errand? Buying chocolates?" asked Shadow.

Jimmy's face turned red. "Um, yes something like that. I've spoken to Ellie Treanor too though. She said Le Vel was the reason Jacqui left Swinegate."

"Are they in a relationship?"

"Not really. Jacqui is mad about him and they go out for dinner now and then, but it seems he isn't willing to commit. Apparently, Jacqui and Ellie have spent quite a few evenings having heart-to-hearts over cocktails on the subject. I get the impression Ellie doesn't entirely approve. She thinks Le Vel's a bit of a slippery character."

"Slippery like a snake," murmured Shadow. He had to admit Jimmy's ability to chat to people wherever he went often drove him mad, but it seemed to be paying dividends when it came to finding out about Le Vel. Making small talk had never been something Shadow excelled at. He'd never seen the need. Maggie was probably the only person outside of work he chatted to and even then, it was mainly one-way traffic from her direction.

"By the way, Chief," said Jimmy interrupting Shadow's thoughts, "there has been a reported sighting of Ling. The piece in last night's *Herald* seemed to do the trick. A guy who was out jogging reported that he saw her on the city walls between Bootham and Monk Bar at about eleven or eleven thirty, so that's after Mrs Chen and the rest of the tour party last saw her. Oh, look Ben and Ollie are already here."

They had arrived in Exhibition Square and Jimmy pointed across the road to where the two forensic scientists, who Shadow privately referred to as Laurel and Hardy, were waiting outside the museum. Shadow groaned when he saw they were already dressed in their bright blue suits and masks and attracting quite a lot of attention from passing motorists and pedestrians.

"I thought you told them to be discreet," he grumbled, as he hurried across the road.

Chapter Four

Down 1.
Norman lost the North so took the South route to find some Italians (6 letters)

ONCE AGAIN DUNNINGTON was waiting for them at the main door of the Eboracum Museum and once again he ushered them quickly inside.

"Ah there you are, Shadow, and I see you've brought the boffins this time too. Excellent! Dr Shepherd is waiting upstairs for you chaps. Now, Shadow, I've arranged for all the staff to come in a little earlier so you can have a chat before we open," he said. "Who do you want to start with?"

"Actually, I have a couple of questions for you, Mr Dunnington," Shadow replied as Jimmy led Ben and Ollie upstairs to the storeroom.

"Righty ho, well fire away," replied Dunnington.

"I understand you spoke to a young Chinese girl, yesterday near the abbey ruins in Museum Gardens."

Dunnington opened his eyes very wide. "Crikey, so you think the Chinese are involved do you? International art thieves maybe? Well no wonder we didn't notice anything.

We didn't stand a chance. Clever bunch the Chinese."

Shadow tried not to let his impatience show on his face or in his voice.

"No, Mr Dunnington, this a different matter entirely. A Chinese tourist has gone missing and we believe you might have spoken to her."

"Come on, Shadow, the place is full of Chinese tourists. How can you expect me to remember all the ones I speak to?"

"She was wearing a pink top with the picture of a cartoon dog on the back and spoke to you quite close to the abbey ruins," Shadow persisted, showing the director the picture he had of Ling.

Dunnington continued to look puzzled for a moment, before realisation dawned on his face. "I do remember now, yes, a quiet, polite little thing. Wanted to know the way to the city walls, so I pointed her in the right direction. Couldn't speak much English, but very grateful, lots of thank yous."

"She didn't say anything else? If she was meeting someone perhaps?"

"No, nothing like that. She just had a tatty old map and kept pointing to Bootham Bar. It was marked with an X."

"Thank you very much, Mr Dunnington. You've been very helpful," replied Shadow. He left the museum director and went to speak to Glenn and Pete the security guards. They were dressed as Roman soldiers once again and were laughing between themselves as they leaned against one of the atrium columns, although they straightened up when Shadow approached.

"Morning, gentlemen. I understand the two of you served together in the army," he said.

"That's right, sir, we were in the Royal Yorks together," replied Pete, who was the taller of the two.

"We got our discharge papers about a year ago," added Glenn, who was roughly a head shorter than his colleague, but equally muscular and tanned. Remembering his conversation with Jake, Shadow glanced down at Glenn's feet. They were indeed oddly small. Their golden-brown skin in the middle of a North Yorkshire winter also bothered him.

"Did you go abroad afterwards?" he enquired. Both soldiers looked puzzled by his question, until Glenn followed his train of thought and smiled.

"No, sir. Steph's got a sun bed she lets us use. You know, so we look more the part."

Shadow nodded at this explanation. The second Mrs Dunnington did indeed sport a similar sun-kissed glow.

"And when did you start working here?" he asked, although thanks to the staff list he already knew the answer.

"About four or five months ago," said Pete.

"Steph told Pete this place was looking for two security guards. We were both between jobs, but we'd been based at Strensall and Catterick before and always had a good time up north, so we thought why not."

"You knew Mrs Dunnington before you started working here?" asked Shadow.

Pete grinned. "Yeh, me and Steph go way back."

Shadow wondered if Mr Dunnington had known this before employing the two soldiers or was he as clueless regarding this matter as he seemed to be about everything else?

"I assume you both know why we are here. We are investigating the theft of several valuable artefacts."

Neither men showed any sign of surprise.

"It didn't happen on our watch," stated Pete decisively and Glenn nodded.

"It must have happened before we got here. They had two old-timers on the door before us. Maybe you should speak to them."

"Have you ever noticed anyone acting suspiciously at all? Trying to take photos of the exhibits perhaps."

Again, both the soldiers shook their heads in unison.

"No way. We'd have stopped them."

"And the storeroom is always locked. They couldn't have got in there."

"The alarms are turned on every night."

"If some had tried to break in, they'd be triggered immediately."

Shadow thanked them for their time. He had to hand it to them, they were well drilled. They had obviously worked out what they were going to say to him and would stick to their story no matter what. Perhaps they had a point though and he should speak to the previous security guards.

He made his way upstairs. Jimmy was in the staff room interviewing the volunteer guides who were patiently waiting outside on a row of chairs. Their average age seemed to be around eighty and Shadow couldn't help noticing one lady had already dozed off with her knitting resting in her lap. He stopped outside Stephanie's door and knocked loudly, hoping she might be able to give him the names of the previous security guards. There was no answer. He knocked again and put his head around the door. He wasn't entirely surprised to see there was no sign of her.

A little further along the corridor he found the forensics team at work in the storeroom where he'd been shown the fake items the previous day.

"How are you getting on in here?"

"Dr Shepherd showed us the fake coins and said we could take one back to the lab and run some tests on it," said Ben.

"Good idea. Any signs of a break-in at all?" Shadow asked without much hope. Both scientists turned to him and shook their heads.

"We've found some prints here on the windowsill and on one of the glass display cases though, Chief," said Ben. Shadow looked at where he was pointing and clearly remembered placing his hands on the sill as he looked out of the window.

"I think you'll probably find those belong to me and Sergeant Chang," he said with a sigh.

"Oh that's a shame," replied Ben looking crestfallen. "Ollie found something interesting though."

His colleague beckoned Shadow over to the window.

"Look outside, Chief. There's a very narrow balcony that runs along the front of the first-floor windows. It's clear here and along to the left, but to the right it's covered in leaves."

"Maybe the wind has blown them that way or it's simply the way they fall from the trees. Have you been outside?"

"Not yet, Chief, I was going to unlock the window, but the key for it isn't here as you can see. I went to ask the lady next door," he explained, pointing to Stephanie's office on the other side of the wall. "She gave me the key out of her window and said all the windows opened with the same key. When I told her I didn't think that was very secure, she got quite cross with me."

Shadow agreed with the scientist for once; so much for Dunnington telling him their security arrangements were state-of-the-art and he could well imagine Stephanie would have very little patience with poor bumbling Ollie.

"Well look outside and see what you can find. I'll meet you downstairs."

Shadow decided to leave them to their work, unconvinced they would discover anything very helpful. Dr Shepherd was waiting outside in the corridor.

"I thought I'd hover around, Chief Inspector, in case you

or your colleagues need to ask me any questions," she said.

"Thank you, Dr Shepherd, that's good of you. As a matter of fact, there is something I wondered if you could help with. Do you have any idea how the thieves would have forged the coins? The actual process I mean. Would you need to have any historical knowledge of how the original coins were made?"

"As you may well imagine, Chief Inspector, I've thought of little else since the theft was discovered. I've done quite a lot of research on the subject and I believe the forgers would have needed to use a combination of an impressed die and a hand-cut die. I think they used the original coins to make a mould, a hub I believe it is called, then added the finer details by hand. It's not a particularly hi-tech procedure, but you would need to be quite highly skilled and of course have a very good eye for detail."

"And all the missing coins were gold?"

"Yes, though possibly one or two may be silver. As I said, since the discovery we have been checking every item in the collection. Naturally the replica coins are only base metal covered in a thin layer of gold," she explained.

Shadow thanked Dr Shepherd, then went downstairs and waited for Jimmy and the two forensic scientists, in an alcove behind the display cabinets. He would be the first to admit that he knew nothing about running a museum, but the set-up here at the Eboracum seemed amateurish to say the least. Two security guards who wear fancy dress and spend most of their time chatting up the female visitors. Volunteers who dozed off. An overworked and disrespected curator and a director's secretary who seemed to have an aversion to her desk. Shadow shook his head. What was Dunnington thinking of? Was he really as incompetent as he seemed? Maybe there was something in Jimmy's idea. The collection was well insured. Could he benefit financially in any way? Perhaps he should check the policy details more closely back at the station.

The museum was open now and visitors were beginning to filter in as Shadow waited for his colleagues. Jimmy was the first to join him, jogging down the stairs two at a time.

"Anything to report?" he asked.

Jimmy shook his head. "Not really, Chief, most of them have been volunteering here for years, but only do a day or two a week at the most. Maud does Mondays and Thursdays, Dennis does alternate Wednesdays, June does Fridays except for the last week in the month when she helps out at the library instead, then there's Colin, he..."

Shadow held up his hand to silence his sergeant.

"All right, all right, I don't need to hear the full timetable. Run their names through the computer when we get back and check none of them have a record. Nothing else?"

"Only that none of them had anything good to say about the new Mrs Dunnington and the changes she's been making. There was a general feeling that the theft would never have happened had Mrs D number one had still been running things."

At that moment, they were joined by Ben and Ollie. Shadow could tell from the disappointed expressions on their faces that they hadn't found anything of note either.

"I take it there's nothing else to report regarding the storeroom?" he asked. The scientists shook their heads in unison, but Ben was the first to speak.

"We don't think the wiring for the alarm has been tampered with. We lifted the floorboards up, but there's a sheet of metal underneath, so we don't think anyone could come up from below. There's metal beneath the attic floor too, so that rules out coming through the ceiling. The doors and windows have security pads on. If they are opened the alarm would sound, but the alarm isn't turned on when the museum is open, so it's possible someone could get in during the day, but they would probably be seen by someone in the staff room or the office next door."

"Or possibly even people eating in the café if the theft occurred during the summer," added Ollie.

Shadow frowned. He was sure the coins must have been stolen from the storeroom. Just standing in the alcove for a few minutes had convinced him that trying to steal from the exhibit rooms risked being seen by too many witnesses. Also, the more he heard, the more certain he was the theft must be an inside job.

"Did you look outside on the balcony?" Shadow asked.

"Yes, Chief, but I couldn't get very far. My feet were too

big. Sorry," apologised Ben.

Shadow glanced down. The scientist's feet were indeed almost clown-like in their size. He turned to the shorter Ollie.

"Couldn't you go out there?"

"I'm scared of heights, Chief."

Shadow sighed and shook his head. Why wasn't he surprised?

Ben started talking again. "But while I was out there, Chief, I did think the clear section of the balcony had been swept clean. There was no bird mess or sticky leaf residue at all. I was going to try and take photos of the section I couldn't get to, but the blonde lady tapped on the window and shouted at me. She accused me of being a peeping Tom. She frightened me half to death."

"He nearly fell off the balcony," confirmed Ollie. "She isn't very patient, is she?"

Shadow had to admit that he wasn't blessed with patience when it came to dealing with Ben and Ollie either, but at least he knew the elusive Stephanie was still somewhere in the museum. He was about to say that it was time they should leave when Tim Dunnington reappeared.

"Shadow, I've got one word for you," he said, looking as if he'd just had the most brilliant idea. "Sniffer dogs!"

"Sniffer dogs?" repeated Shadow, not entirely sure where this conversation was going and holding himself back from pointing out that that was two words.

"Yes, you need them on the case. We used them in the army for sniffing out bombs. They'll find the missing stuff in no time," Dunnington insisted.

Shadow ignored the sniggers coming from Ollie and Ben and wondered whether it was worth explaining that even the keenest canine nose would have difficulty tracking coins, which as far as he knew had no scent and may well have disappeared months ago. However, Dunnington clearly wasn't expecting a response and was prattling on again.

"Now if you are all done, gentlemen, do pop into our café for some refreshments. No point loitering here for everyone to see," he said. "We've had a bit of a revamp and gone for an Asian fusion theme in there. It's quite new for us. All Steph's idea—she's all for trying new things. We ate stacks of the stuff on our honeymoon. It's important to keep up with the times and she certainly stops me being an old fuddy-duddy."

Before Shadow could say that they were about to leave, Jimmy, Ben and Ollie were already heading through the café door, so with a sigh of resignation, he trudged after them. When he entered the room, his nostrils were hit by an array of unusual and exotic smells. Personally, he thought café with its elegant architecture and terrace overlooking Museum Gardens would have better lending itself to serving traditional afternoon teas with sandwiches and scones, but perhaps with all their visitors from abroad, Stephanie had a point.

The young chef in a white overall, who must have been

primed by Dunnington, hurried over with a tray of small plates of food and placed them on a table for them along with four glasses and a bottle of mineral water. Shadow peered at a plate of fried chicken pieces in a red sauce. He sniffed and guessed it was sweet and sour. He took one and with slight trepidation popped it in his mouth. Immediately he regretted it. His tongue felt like it was on fire. If he'd been in a cartoon, steam would be shooting out of his ears.

"Is it hot, Chief?" asked Ben, who was never one to miss an opportunity to ask a question with an obvious answer. Shadow exhaled loudly as he swallowed down the food with great difficulty.

"Thermal or chemical?" asked Ollie.

"Both," replied Shadow in a strangled voice, gulping down a glass of water Jimmy had handed to him.

"Oh, great we love spicy food, don't we, Ben?"

Shadow watched as the scientist popped a piece of chicken in his mouth and ate it with ease before declaring to his colleagues, "Bang bang chicken with firecracker sauce. Delish!"

Shadow scowled. If he'd know it was called that he would never have even tried it. Jimmy and the other two enthusiastically tucked in, as Shadow sipped the water and nursed his burning throat. He didn't care how fashionable this Asian fusion stuff was, they should definitely have stuck to cream teas in his opinion. He decided to leave his more adventurous colleagues and went in search of the elusive

Stephanie once more.

Out in the atrium, Dr Shepherd was talking to the volunteers, directing some to their positions and thanking the others for coming in on their day off. A school party of overexcited children had arrived and were all vying to have a photo taken with Glenn and demanding to hold his spear. There was no sign of Pete.

Shadow went upstairs and turned towards the corridor where the offices and storeroom were situated. Suddenly the staff room door opened and out stepped Stephanie and Pete. Shadow ducked behind one of the columns and watched. Both were hastily rearranging their clothing. They exchanged a quick kiss before Stephanie went back into her office and Pete strode down the corridor to where Shadow was hiding. He remained out of sight until the soldier had passed by, then waited a few seconds longer before heading towards the staff room. He pushed open the door. It was unlocked. Inside several armchairs were arranged in a semicircle with a coffee table in the middle. There was a sink and a table beneath the window, holding a kettle, several slightly chipped mugs, an open carton of milk and a tin marked 'biscuits'. In the corner was another door. Shadow tried to open it, but it was locked. Aware of the fairly lax security arrangements at the museum, he set about searching for a key. In less than two minutes, he discovered one, hanging on a hook beneath the sink, and sure enough when he tried it in the lock, it fitted perfectly.

When he opened the door, he found a small room, not much bigger than a cupboard. There was a window with a sheet hung up to act like a makeshift curtain. Two chairs held neatly folded men's clothing. It was obviously where Pete and Glenn got changed into their Roman costumes. There was also the faint hint of a woman's perfume in the air and a few stray long blonde hairs on the dark blue carpet. Shadow didn't need his forensics team to tell him what had been going on there. He couldn't say he was exactly shocked, but he was surprised at how blatant Stephanie and Pete were in their behaviour.

He locked the door and replaced the key before leaving the staff room and knocking on Stephanie's door.

"Yeh what?" came the response. Shadow opened the door and stepped inside.

"Sorry to bother you, Mrs Dunnington," he began politely.

Stephanie looked up from filing her already immaculate red talons. "Oh not you again! What do you want this time?"

"Just the names of the previous two security guards who worked here, please. If it's not too much trouble."

His request resulted in another hair toss and eye roll, but she did at least spin her chair around and open a drawer in the filing cabinet. The talons tapped as she flicked through the folders before finally extracting a sheet of paper and handing it over to Shadow.

"Is that it?"

Shadow glanced down and read the two names and addresses she had provided.

"Yes, as ever thank you for your help, Mrs Dunnington," he replied as he left her office, but Stephanie had already returned to her nails.

WHEN HE FINALLY managed to get his younger colleagues to leave the museum's café, Shadow decided he and Jimmy should take a walk along the city walls. According to the one report they had from a member of the public, this was the last place Ling had been seen.

The two detectives joined the city walls by climbing up the narrow steps alongside Bootham Bar. York's stone walls still encircled the oldest part of the city. There were four gates, each at roughly the four points of the compasses, so it was possible to climb up and walk along the ramparts. What had once been York's main defence against marauding Scots and rampaging Vikings was now just another tourist attraction. Visitors walked along, stopping here and there to admire the view or take a photo, where once boiling oil poured down and arrows were fired at any would-be invaders.

Shadow glanced down longingly as they passed the steps leading down to The Lamb and Lion beer garden, but sadly it was still too early for lunch. Jimmy's phone launched into a chorus of bleeps and pings again as they walked along.

"Anything?" asked Shadow.

"Some news from the Chinese embassy, Chief. There is a report of a Ling Li who has gone missing from Shanghai. Apparently, Ling is twenty years old and worked near the Jing'an Temple for a jeweller and she told her employer a few days ago that she was ill and couldn't come to work. He hasn't heard from her since. He went to her home, but there was no sign of her. If she is missing, then she's the second girl from the area to disappear. About three months ago Mei Wu, who was also in her twenties and employed as a gold-smith was seen getting on a plane, but nobody has heard from her since. She told the taxi driver who took her to the airport that she was going to Hong Kong to meet her boyfriend. Both girls were from poor farming families. They moved to the city to work in the jewellery trade."

"Did the girls know each other?" asked Shadow. Jimmy scrolled through the email on his screen.

"They don't think so, but it's possible."

"Anything else?"

After more scrolling, Jimmy finally replied.

"When Mei was reported missing, the police searched her apartment and found her passport. They checked with the airline and it turns out she travelled under the name Denise Wong and used a passport in the same name. It was a BNO passport."

"BNO?" queried Shadow.

"British National Overseas. Any Hong Kong resident could register to be a BNO if they were citizens before the 1997 transfer of power to China. Loads of my mum's friends who still live over there have got BNO passports," explained Jimmy.

"Did the Hong Kong police try and track down the real Denise Wong?" asked Shadow.

"Yes, but she wasn't at her last known address and they haven't been able to find her," replied Jimmy after more scrolling. "What's more Mei, travelling as Denise, didn't stay in Hong Kong. She took another flight from there to London."

"Are they sure it was Mei?"

"Yes, apparently after she was reported missing, they tracked her through airport CCTV for that day. They also contacted the NCA when they knew she was heading to the UK."

Shadow nodded. The NCA or National Crime Agency not only dealt with organised crime and drug trafficking, but human trafficking too. The two detectives walked a little further along in silence as Shadow processed the information and Jimmy set about generating theories.

"Maybe Mei and Ling are friends and they just decided to move over here. Maybe they were running away from something back home; that's why they didn't tell anyone. Mei could be here in York and Ling could have come to join her, but that doesn't explain why Mei used a false passport.

Or they could have committed a crime and be running away. Or maybe Mei did have a boyfriend, but he was British, so she came over here with him then Ling came over here to join her, but there's no mention of her meeting a man at the airport and I suppose we can't be sure Mei came to York."

Shadow let him chatter on without responding, while he thought.

"Do we know what plane Ling is meant to have arrived on in London?"

"I'll check," replied Jimmy, who began tapping at his phone immediately. As they turned the North Corner, where the wall widened, they came across a very noisy hen party squealing in delight as they posed with Glenn and Pete from the museum.

"Those two get about a bit don't they?" commented Shadow under his breath as he edged past.

"They certainly seem popular with the ladies don't they, Chief," replied Jimmy. Shadow nodded recalling Maggie had said something similar about Le Vel.

"And who's providing security at the museum while those two are busy entertaining the tourists up here?"

"Maud said one of the volunteers usually covers for them for about half an hour before lunch. Apparently, it's all part of the marketing plan, having them hand out leaflets as they walk the walls. Do you remember Dr Shepherd said something similar? They help the museum get quite a few visitors in the afternoon that way," explained Jimmy.

Perhaps they did, thought Shadow, but he couldn't see Maud and her volunteers were an adequate replacement for two ex-soldiers. Did whoever steal the coins know that? Did they wait until Glenn and Pete were out of the way? He told Jimmy about seeing Stephanie and Pete leave the staff room. His sergeant looked shocked.

"That's awful! Poor Mr Dunnington, they've only been married a few months."

Shadow didn't reply. Personally, he thought what goes around comes around. Tim Dunnington had been unfaithful to his wife of over twenty years and now his new wife was treating him the same way. Jimmy paused at a section of the wall roughly halfway between Bootham Bar and Monk Bar.

"It was about here that we have the last report of Ling being seen," he said. Shadow looked around them. To the left it was possible to look into the dean's private garden and to the right were steps that led down to Grays Court, but at this time of year they were locked. In the summer months, the walls would be packed with tourists, but today the stretch they were on was deserted. They were lucky to have received any sightings of Ling. At the sound of heavy foot-steps behind him, Shadow turned around. Pete and Glenn had caught up with them.

"Do you two walk this way at the same time every day?" asked Shadow.

"Yeh roughly," replied Glenn.

"Weather permitting," added Pete.

"Were you here yesterday? Did you see this girl?" Jimmy asked holding up his phone showing the image of Ling.

Both men peered at the screen but shook their heads.

"I don't think so," said Glenn.

"I can't remember to be honest. We see loads of tourists," agreed Pete.

Shadow wondered if the two men ever disagreed. There was a sudden gust of wind and the sun disappeared behind a dark cloud.

"I think we'll be heading back now, if that's all, Chief Inspector," said Glenn pulling his flapping cloak a little tighter around his shoulders. Shadow thanked the two men and watched for a moment as they walked back in the direction of the museum. He and Jimmy carried on towards Monk Bar. As they drew level with the back of the shops in Monk Bar Court, they could see the builders working on the last two empty shops in the row. There was a loud burst of laughter. Shadow peered down to where the builders were standing next to the cement mixer and chatting to Le Vel.

"Ah good one, Paul mate, you always crack me up," said one the builders.

"You keep up the good work, lads, and remember: call in whenever you want and one of the girls will make you a cuppa," replied Le Vel as he left them with a cheery wave. As Shadow watched them the first cold drops of sleety rain fell from the leaden sky.

"You see, he's friendly with everyone. Come on, Chief,

let's go," said Jimmy, who was already shivering again. They ducked under the low stone entrance to the gatehouse of Monk Bar. However, instead of heading down the steep steps, Jimmy pointed to the open door opposite with a wooden hand-painted sign saying, 'Monk Bar Café'.

"Hey, we could try here, Chief. Mum was telling me about it. They've opened recently and are meant to do great coffee," he suggested and disappeared through the door before giving his boss a chance to respond. Shadow was starting to get tired of being railroaded into eateries he had no wish to visit, but with a sigh he followed his sergeant.

The café was situated in the rooms above the arched gateway of the fourteenth-century bar. Its stone walls and floors had once provided access to the arrow slits and murder holes used by citizens of York to defend themselves from invading enemies. Now, it was full of pine chairs and tables covered in checked cloths and eclectic pieces of artwork hung on the walls. It looked and sounded as though the kitchen was situated in the upper levels along with the city's only working portcullis, although Shadow knew this hadn't been lowered since the Queen's coronation.

As soon as they entered, a large lady with spiky white hair and thick round glasses bustled over to them and placed two menus down on the table.

"Hello there, gentlemen, my name is Genevieve. Have a little look at our menu then pop over to the counter and let me know what you'd like," she said with a beaming smile.

Shadow frowned. He wasn't a huge fan of coffee unless it was an espresso in one of his favourite Italian restaurants. His sergeant, however, was quite the aficionado.

"I'll have a ham sandwich and a beer," Shadow announced without bothering to look at the menu.

"Oh, they don't have a licence and it's a vegetarian place," said Jimmy.

Shadow scowled. If his sergeant had told him this, he would never have followed him through the door.

"Fine, a cheese sandwich and a cup of tea then," he replied wearily.

"Earl Grey or lapsang souchong?"

"Just Yorkshire." He couldn't believe he'd bypassed The Lamb and Lion for this place.

"I think I'm going to have the avocado on toast and a Colombian coffee," said Jimmy.

Shadow continued to chunter as he put on his glasses and frowned at the menu in his hand.

"And they've forgotten to print the prices on here."

"Oh, that's something else, Chief. You just pay whatever you think the meal is worth. It's up to you."

Shadow shook his head.

"They'll be bankrupt in a week," he muttered.

"Maybe people are more honest than you give them credit for, Chief."

"How long have you been in the police?" Shadow asked incredulously and Jimmy grinned.

"Well, I still think it's a great idea," he replied.

"Yes, Sergeant, but you aren't their accountant."

Jimmy went to the counter to place their order with Genevieve. Shadow tutted quietly to himself as he flicked through the menu that the blurb on the back told him was printed on paper from a sustainable source and was also fully recyclable. As he read on, he also learnt the owner's full name was Genevieve Knott. The Knotts were one of the city's most prominent Quaker families. Back in Victorian times, along with the more famous Rowntrees and Terrys, they had begun making chocolate, the product York was most famous for. The Knotts had sold their business to a multinational confectionery company several years ago, but most of the family remained in the city. Shadow put the menu back on the table. No wonder Genevieve wasn't too concerned about this place making a profit.

On the wall next to him there was a metal vintage sign advertising 'Knotts Chocolate-Covered Almonds', the company's most famous product. There were also framed photographs of the proprietor in various exotic locations. In one it looked like she was in a rainforest; in another she was posing outside a Chinese temple. Jimmy returned to the table and looked at the photos his boss was studying.

"Hey that's a coincidence," he said.

"What is?" asked Shadow.

"There's a picture of the Jing'an Temple in Shanghai."

Shadow pushed his glasses further on his nose as he

squinted at the image more closely.

"Is it just me being suspicious again, Sergeant, or are we encountering rather a few too many coincidences? Colchester Museum discovers the coins are fakes and Pete the new security guard just happens to come from Essex, a girl from Shanghai goes missing and we meet Le Vel who exports to China and now here's a picture of a Shanghai temple."

"Come on, Chief, coincidences happen. Colchester has got a big army base and Pete used to be a soldier. We only stumbled across Le Vel when we went to see Jacqui Heaton. He isn't involved; you just don't like him." Jimmy pointed to the photo on the wall. "As for this, everyone who goes to Shanghai probably takes a picture of the temple. It's like coming to York and photographing the Minster."

"Fascinating city, Shanghai," said a loud voice behind them. It was Genevieve carrying their order on a tray. She placed it down heavily, causing Shadow's tea to slop into the saucer as she chattered on. "I first went there with my dear late father on an almond-buying trip. I go there now to source the best tea for this place. The stalls surrounding the temple are incredible and also where I found Pendle." She gestured to a small grey dog with one eye and only three legs. He was sniffing intently at Shadow's ankle.

"It can't have been easy to transport a dog over here from China," remarked Shadow edging his foot away from the canine's nose, as Jimmy bent down to ruffle the unfortunate creature's ears.

"He needed rescuing and you can't let a bit of paperwork

and red tape get in the way of doing what's right, Chief Inspector, but I like the way your policeman's brain works," said Genevieve as Shadow wondered how she knew his rank, let alone the fact that he was in the police. "That's what I wanted to talk to you about. A group of friends and I often put on a murder mystery evening and the two of you would be the perfect addition. Two real-life detectives."

Genevieve beamed at him as Shadow cringed inwardly. He could think of little he would enjoy less.

"Actually that sounds like a lot of fun," replied Jimmy as Shadow scowled at him. Of course, his sergeant had probably told her his life story while he went to place the order. "I've never been to a murder mystery evening before. Sophie, my girlfriend would probably enjoy it too. She's a pathologist."

"Even better!" exclaimed Genevieve clapping her hands in delight. As she did so, Shadow noticed a gold charm bracelet jangling on her wrist. Amongst the charms was one of the she-wolf with the twins, the symbol of Rome. *Simply another coincidence?* wondered Shadow. Fortunately, at that moment a group of unsuspecting Chinese tourists arrived, and Genevieve swooped over to them.

"*Nee how!*" she declared loudly. Shadow cringed. Her pronunciation was even worse than his. As she showed them to the table next to the detectives, she grinned at Jimmy. "I've been learning online, ready for my next visit."

"Very good, Miss Knott," he replied politely, as Shadow took a bite of his slightly stale cheese sandwich and made a private resolution to never let Jimmy choose where they ate again. Over in the corner a young couple were using their phones to photograph their lunch. Shadow nodded in their direction.

"Do you think they're here to review the place?" he quietly asked his sergeant.

Jimmy glanced over and shook his head. "No, they're probably just going to put a post on their Facebook or Instagram accounts, Chief."

"Why?"

"Well, that's what people do with social media isn't it? You share pictures of meals, or where you go on holiday, with your friends or followers."

Shadow looked down at his rather unappetising lunch and shook his head. Even if he possessed close friends, he couldn't imagine anyone would be interested in seeing a picture of this sandwich.

"The world's gone mad," he grumbled. "Does nobody have a private life anymore?"

After lunch, they made their way back to the station. Jimmy's phoned bleeped as they walked down Stonegate. He tapped the screen and read the message out loud.

"There was a delayed flight from Shanghai to Heathrow that morning. It was two hours late due to bad weather, Chief. They've emailed me a list of all passengers. Ling Li isn't on the list, but there is another name."

"Denise Wong by any chance?"

"Yes, Chief."

CHAPTER FIVE

Down 4.
A pound, euro or dime to pay in company partly (4 letters)

B ACK AT THE station, one of the small incident rooms
had been set up for the two investigations. There were a
handful of desks and a few whiteboards. Only a couple of
uniformed officers were present and they were both manning
the phones, taking calls from members of the public with
reports of seeing young Chinese women, who on closer
investigation weren't Ling.

"Is it my imagination or are we a little short-handed?"
asked Shadow as he shrugged off his old wax jacket and
draped it on the back of the nearest chair.

"It's February half-term, Chief. A lot of the officers with
children have taken the week off," explained Jimmy.

"I could help, sir," offered Tom eagerly, appearing from
behind one of the whiteboards he'd wheeled into the room.

"Shouldn't you be somewhere else?" Shadow asked
slightly sceptically.

"I've been assigned to help Sergeant Hedley in the records office, but he doesn't seem to like me touching

anything. He sent me down here to help."

"Fine, well unless you are fluent in Chinese, you can concentrate on the museum theft. Sergeant Chang will give you the list of volunteers at the museum. Run them through the computer and make sure none of them are criminal masterminds in disguise. Do the same with Pete and Glenn, the two new security guards. See what you can find out about their time in the army. Then check and see if any other museums have reported similar thefts in the last few years."

Tom scurried away eagerly and Shadow turned to Jimmy. "As we didn't get any other helpful responses to Ling's disappearance from *The Herald*, get on to the press office at HQ, see if they can get her picture on the television news."

"No problem, Chief. Then I thought I'd look and see if either of the missing girls from Shanghai have got a Weibo account."

"What on earth is that?"

"It's like the Chinese version of Facebook or Twitter. You know social media, like I was telling you about in the café. I thought Ling or Mei might have posted something."

Shadow wasn't entirely sure he did know, but he was prepared to defer to Jimmy on this point. He sat down at one of the empty desks with a telephone. Even if Jimmy's theory of the theft being an insurance scam was inspired, by the plot of a Hollywood film, it wouldn't hurt to find out what financial position the museum was in. With a heavy heart he put a call into the accountant and museum trustee Jonty Woodhead. Jonty was well suited to his profession. He treated every conversation as if it was a transaction, carefully weighing up if the details should be listed under assets or liabilities in the balance sheet of his mind.

"I'm really not sure I should speak to you without first taking Rutherford's counsel," the accountant hedged after much humming and hawing. Shadow raised his eyes to the ceiling, he knew he shouldn't have bothered phoning him.

"All I can tell you," Jonty carried on, "is that the museum is a registered charity. A charity by definition is to be of benefit to the public, not necessarily to make a profit."

Shadow took that to mean the place wasn't making money, but he knew the careful accountant wouldn't tell him any more, so he thanked him for his time and hung up. It seemed insurance fraud was still a possibility, but would Dunnington take such a risk? And if not him, who?

His next call was to the National Crime Agency. After being transferred several times, then put on hold for at least ten minutes, he was finally put through to Inspector Saskia Grabowski, who had spoken to the Chinese authorities about the missing Mei Wu. He briefly told her what had happened with Ling Li's disappearance.

"Have you discovered anything that makes you think the two women are connected?" he asked. He could hear Inspector Grabowski sigh, before she replied.

"It's possible, Chief Inspector, but to be honest we think

there could be thousands of Chinese nationals living here illegally. Some are here for economic reasons, some for political ones, others have been trafficked by snakehead gangs and are exploited terribly when they get here. You'll remember the Morecambe Bay disaster?"

Shadow did remember the dreadful story of how at least twenty-one Chinese illegal immigrant workers had drowned while picking cockles in the bay. It also transpired they had been paid only a £1 a day.

"Are you investigating any cases in North Yorkshire currently?" he asked.

"No, but it's probably happening in most towns and cities. Sometimes it feels like we are fighting a losing battle. I'll make a note of Ling's name and details. If I hear anything, I'll let you know, Chief Inspector."

As he was finishing his conversation with Inspector Grabowski, Shadow could see Tom telling Jimmy something. Not for the first time, Shadow was relieved his sergeant didn't play poker. He was incapable of hiding his emotions. Whatever Jimmy had been told had clearly disappointed him.

"Problem?" Shadow asked as he put down the receiver.

"I checked the museum staff like you asked, sir," began Tom enthusiastically. "They are all clean. Pete and Glenn both enlisted at sixteen, straight from school and after ten years' service were each given an honourable discharge. Then I checked the museums. Only one reported theft of an exhibit in the last four years. Chester Museum had a musket dating from the time of the Civil War stolen about three years ago. They never found out who took it, but it was recovered after it was used in an armed robbery in Liverpool."

Shadow frowned.

"That sounds like it was stolen to order, but I can't see a connection between an old firearm and our stolen coins."

"No." Jimmy sighed. "Except before she came to the Eboracum Museum, Dr Shepherd was curator at the Chester Museum. The police interviewed her as the theft took place only a month after she'd left. She had an alibi for the night the musket was taken. She was at a murder mystery event in Suffolk, at Camilla Dunnington's mother's house." Jimmy paused. "It might just be another coincidence, Chief."

Shadow paused for a moment while he processed this information. As much as his sergeant didn't want Dorothy to be involved, could the thefts from both of Dr Shepherd's most recent places of employment be down to more than bad luck? It was also strange that the ex-wife of her new boss should be the one to provide her with an alibi for the first crime. He turned to Tom and the constables manning the phones.

"Somebody get me the number for Camilla Dunnington in Suffolk," he ordered. A few minutes later he was holding a receiver to his ear again, listening to it ring. A woman's voice answered. Shadow introduced himself, but before he could check whom he was speaking to and explain what his call was about, the woman interrupted him.

"Ah, Chief Inspector Shadow, I thought I might be hearing from you. I take it you want to discuss the theft of the Roman coins from the Eboracum Museum?"

"Yes, when did you hear about it, Mrs Dunnington?"

"Oh a couple of days ago. I'm still in regular contact with Maud and Dennis and a few of the old gang. Now as much as I would like to help you, Chief Inspector, I was just on my way out when you called. I run a local history group in our village hall, and I hate to be late. Perhaps we could schedule another time to chat? How about tomorrow at 9am? Let's make it a Zoom meeting. I always think it's best to talk face to face whenever possible, don't you?"

Shadow covered the mouthpiece with his hand.

"She said she wants to Zoom. Can we do that?" he whispered to Jimmy. His sergeant grinned and gave him a thumbs up. Shadow cleared his throat and confidently replied, "Yes that will be fine, Mrs Dunnington. I'll look forward to speaking with you tomorrow."

"What on earth's a Zoom meeting?" he asked as soon as he put the phone back down.

"It's only like having a video call, Chief. Don't worry, I'll get it set up for you," Jimmy reassured him.

Shadow stood up and shook his head. People said technology was there to make life easier; he found it made his more complicated. He stepped out into the corridor where one of the station's many temperamental coffee machines was situated. He pressed the necessary buttons then waited for the machine to splutter and gurgle into action. Back in the incident room he could hear Jimmy and Tom chatting.

"So you didn't fancy getting away for some winter sun too, Tom?"

"No, not really. I'm not a big fan of sitting on the beach. My skin's too pale; I always get sunburnt and peel."

"It's meant to be good for you. Not getting burnt but sitting in the sun I mean. Sophie was telling me about people getting ill because of lack of sunlight. SAD, seasonal affective disorder—that's what they call it. She said it can make you miserable, more irritable, less sociable."

"Do you think that's what's wrong with the chief?"

"No, he's the same even when it's sunny."

Out in the corridor Shadow rolled his eyes as he collected his coffee.

"I've left the room, not lost my hearing," he bellowed. "Don't make me regret letting you work here before you've even begun, Tom."

He decided to leave Jimmy and Tom in the incident room and take his cup of disappointing brown liquid to pay his old friend George a visit. Sergeant George Hedley was up in the records office and had worked at the station longer than anyone else. There wasn't much that had happened in the city over the last forty years that he didn't know about. The only downside was he worked in the top of the old

Guildhall tower, which meant Shadow was usually exhausted by the time he climbed up the stairs to reach him.

"What can you tell me about Ernest Level?" he asked as he flopped down in the chair opposite his old friend.

"Honest Ernie?" George laughed, but Shadow looked at him blankly. "Don't you remember those terrible adverts he used to do on local radio? 'If you want to sell your unwanted gold for the best price, come to Honest Ernie. He's always on the level'." George tunelessly sang the jingle, but Shadow was still none the wiser.

"I'm not really a fan of local radio," he replied. "So he didn't only deal old and rare coins."

"No, he dabbled in jewellery, old stamps, some antiques—anything he could get his hands on. He was what we used to call a bit of a 'wheeler dealer'. Larger than life and not just physically. You'd see him whizzing around in his red sports car, the top down no matter the weather so everyone could see him. Always had a big, fat cigar clamped in his mouth and some young woman or other by his side."

"Do you know why he left York?"

"From what I heard at the time, it could have been for any number of reasons: customers who felt they'd been cheated, disgruntled business associates, irate husbands. He was quite the ladies' man you know."

"So I hear," replied Shadow, thinking that it sounded like Le Vel junior had inherited several of his father's characteristics. George got up and wandered over to a shelf of files.

He ran a finger along them before selecting one and pulling it out. He began flicking through.

"Ah yes I thought so," he said looking up and peering at Shadow over his glasses. "Not long after he disappeared West Midlands got in touch with us. They were trying to track him down. They wanted to talk to him in connection with some fake gold sovereigns that had turned up in the jewellery quarter."

"Did anything come of it?"

George read on a little further and shook his head. "No, it doesn't look like it. It was rumoured he was in Hong Kong, but he was never found."

Before he left Shadow asked George about the two names of the ex-security guards Stephanie had given to him.

"I thought they rang a bell," said Shadow.

"So they should," replied George. "They're ex-coppers. They both used to work here, took early retirement about ten years ago. Nice lads and as honest as they come. I caught up with them for a pint about a month ago. Neither were very happy with being dismissed from the museum I can tell you."

"They were dismissed?"

"Yes, by the 'blonde bimbo' as they called her."

"Ah the new Mrs Dunnington strikes again," said Shadow with a wry smile.

"That's her—Miss Roper that was," replied George.

"Do you know her?"

"Know of her. She's Tony Roper's daughter. Hadn't you heard?"

Shadow looked at his old friend in surprise. Tony Roper was a well-known criminal. He was the closest thing North Yorkshire had ever had to a gangster. He'd been involved in everything from armed robberies to extortion. About ten years ago, he'd been sent down for a twenty-two-year stretch. Harrogate had been the base for most of his activities, but Shadow had given evidence in his trial regarding an attempted bank robbery in York.

"When Tony was put away, Stephanie and her mum Sharon went back down south," George continued. Shadow nodded as he recalled an attractive blonde woman who had been led away sobbing when Tony's sentence was read out. Well, that at least went some way to explaining Stephanie's animosity towards him and his colleagues. She would only have been a teenager when her father was taken away from her.

"Where's Roper now?" he asked.

"The last I heard he'd been moved up here to Full Sutton after attempting to break out of Chelmsford, but that was over a year ago."

Shadow stood up to leave. Perhaps that explained why Stephanie had returned to York. Full Sutton was a category-A prison about twelve miles out of the city. Maybe she wanted to be close to her father. Suddenly, a thought occurred to him.

"Do you know if Ernie Level and Roper were associates, George?"

The sergeant removed his glasses and rubbed his eyes as he often did when thinking.

"Not that I can recall, but I suppose it's possible. Ernie left the city not long after Roper's trial, but I don't know if there was a definite connection."

Shadow thanked George and as he left the records office, he wondered if Stephanie's dislike of the police was the only trait she shared with her father. Was she still in touch with members of the criminal fraternity? Was her father's prison move the only reason she had returned to Yorkshire?

BACK DOWN IN the incident room, Jimmy was watching the early evening news on his laptop. Shadow sat down in the chair next to him. The lead story on the national news was about a gang of people smugglers, who were due to be sentenced after thirty-nine Vietnamese migrants had been found dead in the back of their refrigerated truck somewhere in Essex. Shadow shuddered. He could think of few worse ways to die than slowly suffocating in the dark and freezing cold. He was reminded of the stories throughout the summer of other illegal migrants—sometimes women and young children risking their lives to cross the Channel in little more than rubber dinghies. They came from all over, from Syria to

Sudan, all hoping for a better life, even if it meant risking their own. He hated the thought that someone in his own city was exploiting these desperate people.

"How long do you think the smuggling gang will get, Chief?" asked Jimmy.

"Not long enough," replied Shadow grimly.

The local bulletin at the end of the news gave a calm and concise report about the disappearance of Ling. Now they could only hope it would provide further leads.

BEFORE SHADOW LEFT the station, he went to his office and made a call to the governor of Full Sutton prison.

"I understand you have Tony Roper staying with you?"

"We did, Chief Inspector, but unfortunately he died of a heart attack about eighteen months ago. He'd only been here a few weeks."

"Really?" asked Shadow. He was slightly surprised that neither he nor George had heard this news.

"Yes, he was moved here after a failed attempted to break out of Chelmsford."

"I don't suppose you can remember if his daughter, Stephanie, ever visited him while he was with you?"

"Yes, I do actually. He told me she had moved up here to be near him. They were very close."

"Do you know why he tried to break out of Chelmsford?

It's only category B and he must have been getting close to being considered for parole."

"I agree it didn't make much sense, but I heard it was something to do with his family. He'd been told his wife was seeing someone on the outside and didn't take too kindly to the news."

"Was it true?"

"I don't think so. It sounded like someone was winding him up. He was known for having a short fuse to say the least. I do know his wife, Sharon, and Stephanie organised his funeral back down in Essex. I saw Sharon there. She was absolutely distraught, but it was a very quiet affair—less than half a dozen mourners including myself and no press."

Could that be the reason why he hadn't heard about the death, thought Shadow as he thanked the governor and ended the call. As he left the station, he kept thinking about the Ropers and wondered how much Dunnington knew about the family he had married into.

CHAPTER SIX

Across 6.
Slowly inch a step towards this country (5 letters)

LATER THAT EVENING, although his meal at La Scuola
Femminile was as delicious as ever, for once Shadow
didn't linger over his risotto or his Barolo. The tables
surrounding him were full of romantic couples and he had
no desire to become part of any impromptu engagement
celebrations. He had a feeling the restaurant owners, Fran-
cesco and Lucia, would be every bit as enthusiastic as Maria
and Gino about a proposal taking place in their establish-
ment. They had even cajoled Marco, their teenage son, into
walking amongst the tables playing romantic melodies on his
violin. He rolled his eyes at Shadow as he passed by his table.

"I hope they're paying you," Shadow whispered to him.

"Ten quid an hour and no chores for the rest of the
week," the young man whispered back with a grin.

When he'd finished his meal, Lucia came to clear his table. After hearing Mrs Chen's comment about Ling, Shadow
realised he'd recently been paying particular attention to
people's hands. He studied Lucia's as she deftly stacked the

empty plates. Her nails were clean and neatly trimmed and her fingers were speckled with the smooth faded scars from burns after years of working in kitchens. Shadow thought back to Mrs Chen's description of Ling's hands. When she had said they were old and ugly, he now thought they probably bore the signs of working with hot metal, as Jacqui Heaton's did, but until they found her, he wouldn't know for sure.

As he left the restaurant and stepped out on to Petergate, a group of young Chinese women passed him by, giggling and taking photos of each other. Since Ling's disappearance he'd also begun studying the many groups of tourists and students in the city. One member of this group was wearing a pale pink top. A flicker of hope shot through him. Maybe she wasn't missing. Perhaps she had met up with some friends. He followed the group as they turned on to Church Street. Unfortunately, they were all wearing face masks. However, when they arrived in St Sampson's Square, they headed into a pizza restaurant, removing the masks as they did so. Shadow had a chance to look at the girl in pink more closely. It wasn't Ling.

Disappointed, he was about to leave the square when he spotted the Roman Bath. It wasn't a pub he often visited as it was usually so busy with tourists. As the name suggested it was built on the site of the Roman bathhouse and it was still possible to go and visit the remains beneath the pub. What had caught Shadow's attention tonight were the two Roman soldiers standing outside the door posing with some American visitors. Shadow waited for the tourists to hand over their generous tips and leave before he approached the ex-soldiers.

"Ave, gentlemen. Working late?" he asked.

"Just earning a few extra quid," replied Glenn easily.

"A bit of beer money," agreed Pete.

"Although apparently having us around is good for business. The punters love having their photo taken with us and we encourage them to go and have a shufti at the old bathhouse, so the landlord gives us our drinks gratis too," added Glenn with a grin.

"Very enterprising." Shadow nodded. They certainly made the most of their costumes, he thought. Talk about moonlighting.

Shadow entered the pub and ordered a pint of John Smith's. He wasn't particularly shocked to see Stephanie perched on a stool at the other side of the bar. She was wearing a short red silk dress and held a glass of prosecco in one hand and a cigarette in the other. The smoking ban had been in place for years, but like her father, Stephanie clearly believed laws were there to be broken. She completely ignored Shadow when he nodded hello to her.

He took a seat by the fire and sipped his pint. The interior of the pub was decorated with Roman-style columns, and paintings featuring scenes of Roman life covered the walls. The pub was busy. Most of the tables were taken and there was a low hum of various conversations accompanied by the crackle and spit of the logs burning in the grate. The genial atmosphere was rudely interrupted by the shrill ring of a mobile phone. Shadow looked up, not at all surprised to find it was Stephanie's. She looked at the screen and pulled a face as she stubbed out her cigarette and flicked her hair, before answering.

"Hi, Timmy. You okay, babe?"

There was a pause.

"No, babe, I told you. I've got a late-night yoga session, then I'm going for a few drinks with the girls."

Another pause.

"No don't wait up, babe. You've been really stressed. Have an early night. I'll see you in the morning. Night night, babe, love you."

She ended the call and the barmaid gave her a knowing look.

"A late-night yoga session, Steph?"

Stephanie took a sip of her wine, before giving a sly smirk.

"Well I used to tell him I was getting my nails done, but then the bloody police went and shut down my usual place, so I had to come up with something else. And I've had to start giving myself a manicure."

As she spoke, she glanced over in the direction of Shadow and gave him a filthy look, as though she held him personally responsible for this terrible inconvenience to her life.

"Why did they close it down?" asked the barmaid.

Stephanie shrugged. "God knows, something stupid about illegal immigrants or the girls who worked there being used as slave labour."

"That's awful," exclaimed the barmaid looking appalled. "Where were the girls from?"—

"Search me, Vietnam, Korea, the Philippines—they all look the same to me," replied Stephanie with a shrug.

Shadow could hardly believe the casual callousness in the way she spoke. He knew the case she referred to, although it was immigration who had closed the place down. The girls working there were about the same age as Stephanie. Any sympathy he may have felt for her losing her father evaporated.

At that moment, Glenn and Pete entered the pub and were immediately surrounded by more tourists, Japanese this time, all wanting to have a photo with them. After more camera clicks and more tips, they joined Stephanie at the bar. Pete flung his arm around her shoulders.

"New dress, Steph?" asked Glenn.

"Not really. Tim bought it for me on our honeymoon in Hong Kong."

"I thought you went to Sydney on your honeymoon."

"We did, but we stopped off in Hong Kong for a few days."

"It's all right for some." The barmaid laughed. "I had to

make do with a weekend in Skegness."

Stephanie shrugged again as she sipped her prosecco. "It's not about where you go; it's about who you're with," she said before planting a kiss on Pete's lips. Shadow swallowed down the last of his pint. He'd seen and heard enough. Dunnington might be a total fool, but nobody deserved to be mocked so publicly.

He stepped out into St Sampson's Square just in time to spot a familiar tall figure with floppy hair ducking into the narrow entrance of Nether Hornpot Lane. What on earth was Jimmy doing heading to the Swinegate Quarter at this time of night? He considered calling out to him but stopped when he heard a laugh coming from the alleyway. A women's laugh. Shadow couldn't see who she was, but his sergeant certainly wasn't alone. He turned sharply on his heel. Whatever was going on, it had nothing to do with him. Was it his imagination, or had Jimmy been a little furtive recently? Usually he was so open and honest, almost to a fault, yet over the last couple of days he'd had the distinct air of someone with a secret to hide. Shadow headed down Parliament Street and turned on to Ousegate deep in thought. As he crossed the bridge, he almost bumped into Sophie who was hurrying out of the small Sainsbury's.

"Oh sorry, Chief. I wasn't looking where I was going," she apologised. There were dark rings under her eyes and she barely raised a smile. Shadow thought she looked exhausted.

"Have you been working late?" he asked.

"Yes, just finished. I thought I'd grab a pint of milk on my way home. I'm going to need all the coffee I can brew to wake me up in the morning. I never thought I'd miss Donaldson," she replied with a yawn.

"Is Jimmy not with you?" Shadow asked casually.

"No he's working late—something about waiting for a call about that missing girl from Shanghai. He's struggling to catch up with them what with the time difference and everything." She paused and her face creased into a frown. "Actually I thought China was ahead of us, but then right now I'm so tired, I'm not even sure of my own name."

"Of course, I won't keep you," replied Shadow. "Goodnight." He watched her go then continued on his way. As he plodded down the steps to the river, he wondered why his honest sergeant had started lying to his girlfriend. He shook his head. Jimmy was right: here he was again, thinking the worst of people. Perhaps that's what thirty years in the police did to you or had he always been naturally suspicious?

IT WAS A clear crisp night and the full moon shone down, reflecting on the water and picking out the gold lettering of his narrow boat's name. When he stepped aboard *Florence*, his first task was to light the wood-burning stove, then he went to the small galley and poured himself a large glass of Valpolicella. He flicked on his ancient stereo, kicked off his shoes, loosened his tie and sank into the sofa as Louis Armstrong's voice filled the boat. He was singing 'Top Hat, White Tie, and Tails' and Shadow was immediately reminded of Fred Astaire singing the same song at Jacqui Heaton's jewellery shop, admittedly at a much louder volume.

He considered some of the recent businesses he'd come into contact with and wondered how they managed to continue trading. Jacqui with her deafening music, Le Vel and his workforce that didn't actually produce anything and Genevieve with her pay what you want café. Then there was Dunnington who seemed to treat the museum like a hobby. Shadow had remembered who Tim Dunnington reminded him of: the countless boys he'd been at boarding school with. They were all the same, not especially bright, but filled with the confidence that came with knowing they'd never really have to work a day in their lives. Their families were wealthy and, thanks to their names, doors would always open for them.

His thoughts switched to Ling. Although the missing girl and Roman coins seemingly had nothing in common other than being reported on the same day, he couldn't help connecting the cases. Dunnington had spoken to her and she'd been seen on the city walls that were frequently patrolled by Glenn and Pete as well as connecting the Monk Bar Café and shops. Then there was Genevieve visiting Shanghai and Le Vel spending time in Hong Kong along with the Dunningtons who'd honeymooned there. Shadow yawned—maybe his imagination was running away with him and it was all purely coincidence.

The next song began to play. Appropriately, it was Ella Fitzgerald singing 'My Funny Valentine'. It was over twenty-five years since he'd celebrated Valentine's, but he could remember that day like it was yesterday. He'd lived in London back then. It had been a Sunday and he'd woken early and gone to the flower market at Covent Garden and bought as many red roses as he could carry and put vases of them throughout *Florence* as a surprise for Luisa when she woke up. He'd even managed to get an arrangement in the tiny bathroom. She had been delighted; he could see her face now. She'd cooked roast lamb for them, and they'd spent the day lazing around drinking red wine and listening to Frank and Ella. Less than a year later she was gone. Killed. Hit by a careless driver.

Shadow sighed as he finished the last of the wine and stood up to go to bed. He hoped one of Jimmy's theories was right and that the girls from Shanghai had left their home for romantic reasons and were living happily and peacefully, but he very much doubted it.

THE NEXT MORNING, Shadow bolted down his breakfast as quickly as he had his two previous evening meals. He wasn't concerned that there would be an impromptu proposal over the bacon and eggs, but he was aware of the first Mrs Dunnington's Zoom proposition and he didn't want to be late.

When he arrived at the incident room in the station, he found that for the second time that week, Jimmy was nowhere to be seen. Instead, Tom was busily tapping away at the computer, before confidently declaring, "Ready when you are, sir!"

Shadow didn't share the young constable's confidence, but nevertheless he took his seat in front of the screen.

"Shall I stay in case you need me, sir?" asked Tom as eager as ever.

"Definitely. I'll need someone to take notes," replied Shadow squinting at the screen while carefully keeping his hands well away from the keyboard.

"Actually, sir, I've set it up so that the meeting will be recorded."

Shadow raised a still-sceptical eyebrow, but to his surprise as Tom pressed a few keys Camilla Dunnington's face flashed up on to his screen. What didn't surprise him was Camilla Dunnington's appearance. She was exactly as he'd imagined her. Sitting at what looked like a kitchen table in her twinset and pearls with a velvet band holding back her hair and wearing just enough make-up to show she cared. There were thousands of women like her up and down the country, sitting on parish councils, organising village fetes and running gymkhanas. Shadow suspected that without them the nation would probably come to a grinding halt.

"Do I just talk normally?" he asked Tom.

"Yes, sir. I'll unmute you," replied Tom, stepping forward and clicking the mouse.

Shadow cleared his throat and tried not to feel self-conscious.

"Good morning, Mrs Dunnington."

"Good morning, Chief Inspector. Now I'm sure you have lots of questions for me, but I've made a list of information I think you might find useful. Shall I rattle through that first then hand over to you?"

"Please do," replied Shadow. Out of the corner of his eye he could see Tom and the other constables smirking at each other. On the screen in front of him Camilla started reading from her list.

"Firstly, the insurance company. I'm sure you have their details, but when I last spoke to their representative, he suggested we upgrade the museum's security system. Now I don't know if that has happened. If it has you may want to check the company they used and make sure none of their employees have criminal records. Are you writing this down, Chief Inspector?"

"No, but we are recording this meeting, Mrs Dunnington," replied Shadow.

"Oh yes. So you are. Jolly good. Now window cleaners. As far as I know the museum is still using the same company we have employed for years, but they don't always send the same team of cleaners—similarly the maintenance company. It could be worth checking who has been sent out over the last year or so. One rotten apple and all that."

Mrs Dunnington looked up from her list with an expectant expression. Clearly it was now Shadow's turn to speak.

"That's all very helpful, Mrs Dunnington, thank you," he said. "Now I would like to ask you about the time Dr Shepherd visited you down in Suffolk. About three years ago I believe?"

"Yes, that's right, Chief Inspector. I was hosting a murder mystery weekend here at my mother's house. Mummy wasn't as weak then; she enjoyed having visitors. Dorothy came down with Genevieve Knott. Gen and I have been friends for years. We were at school together."

"Here in York?" asked Shadow.

"Yes, I was a boarder at The Mount from the age of eight. Daddy was often posted abroad you see. Gen was a day girl of course," replied Camilla referring to the Quaker all-girls' school. "I'm sure you are looking for a link with this theft and that business with the musket in Chester, but I can assure you that Dorothy—along with everyone else employed at the museum when I was there—went through a very thorough screening process. I checked all references myself. Obviously, I can't speak for those employed since I left the museum." She paused for a moment and briefly adjusted the velvet hair band. "Now I know what you are thinking, Chief Inspector. I'm the wronged ex-wife with an axe to grind; however, that simply isn't the case. I gave Tim and his museum over twenty years of my life, but at the end of this conversation, I don't intend to waste another second on him or it. He's made his bed, so he can jolly well lie in it and with whom is no longer any concern of mine. Goodbye, Chief Inspector, and good luck."

With that Camilla disappeared from his screen and Shadow moved aside to let Tom close down the connection for him. Shadow turned to look at the two whiteboards. The one for the Ling investigation now had a photo of Mei Wu—the other missing girl from Shanghai—together with brief details of where and when they were both last seen.

"Sergeant Chang thought if there's a chance Mei is here in York, having a photo of her was a good idea," Tom explained. Shadow nodded, only half listening. On the board for the museum were photos of Dunnington, Dorothy, Stephanie and the security guards Glenn and Pete. Shadow thought back to Stephanie's conversation that he'd overheard in the pub the previous evening. He was so deep in thought that he didn't notice Jimmy had arrived in the incident room.

"Morning, Chief, how did the Zoom meeting with Camilla Dunnington go?" he asked.

"I'm seriously considering handing the case over to her. She'll probably have more success than us," grumbled Shadow. He paused for a moment and sniffed. "Why can I smell chocolate?"

Jimmy self-consciously raised the sleeve of his jacket to his nose.

"Um I think it's me, Chief. I called into the shop on Swinegate and they were in the middle of making a batch of truffles," he replied.

"How many chocolates do you think Sophie can eat?" asked Shadow.

Jimmy looked a little flustered and quickly changed the subject. "So, what did Camilla say?"

"It turns out she and Genevieve Knott are old school friends. She was adamant that nobody she employed at the museum could be involved in the theft." He turned his attention back to the whiteboards. "But despite her assurances, it doesn't change the fact that when Stephanie and Dunnington were on what must have been a long honeymoon if they went to Australia, Dorothy would have been left in charge of the museum. Which reminds me—" he picked up a marker pen and added Stephanie and Tim's names to the board for the missing Chinese girls along with Genevieve's and Le Vel's "—these four have all visited Shanghai or Hong Kong recently," he said ignoring the heavy sigh coming from Jimmy's direction.

"Sorry, sir, are we saying the two cases are connected?" asked Tom looking confused.

"Possibly," replied Shadow.

"Oh come on, Chief!" said Jimmy in an unusually exasperated tone. "Okay I know Le Vel sells his chocolates to businesses in China and he lived in Hong Kong, but he isn't connected to the museum at all."

"Perhaps not, Sergeant, but I still keep coming back to the fact that his father dealt in old coins," persisted Shadow.

"So? I've got friends whose dads are dentists. It doesn't mean I'd let them pull my teeth out, Chief."

Shadow sighed. He knew Jimmy had a point, but he couldn't shake the feeling that Le Vel was involved somehow. Surely after thirty years of working in the police, he should be able to trust his instincts.

"Humour me, Sergeant. Heaven knows I've humoured enough of your theories. Let's just say I have a hunch about Le Vel. He knows Hong Kong, China and old coins. He's also close to Jacqui who is a jeweller, he's got a van, he's more than capable of charming young impressionable girls."

Jimmy began to protest again and Shadow held up his hands.

"I know, I know he isn't connected to the museum." Shadow paused and frowned before turning to Tom.

"Take that list of volunteers up to Sergeant Hedley and ask him to read through it and see if he knows if any of them were connected to Le Vel or his father. For all we know Maud could turn out to be his great-aunt or second cousin," he said. George was bound to know, but Shadow wasn't prepared to climb all those stairs twice in one week.

Tom scurried away with the list, leaving Shadow and

Jimmy in an uncomfortable silence. It was rare for Jimmy to disagree openly with him; in fact Shadow couldn't recall another occasion. Something strange was definitely going on with his young colleague. Rather than reprimanding him, Shadow decided to keep him busy instead.

"Look, why don't you chase up the insurance company and see if the Eboracum Museum have placed a claim yet. Then check what happened with that nail bar that was closed down by immigration. Make sure the owners haven't managed to open somewhere else. After that go and speak to the Chinese tour party again. They leave for Edinburgh today, don't they?"

"Yes, Chief," replied his sergeant with a nod of his head, but he didn't quite meet Shadow's eye.

Shadow decided to retreat to his office. He sank into his chair and rummaged through his desk drawers for indigestion tablets. All this hurried eating and being upset with Jimmy was playing havoc with his stomach. As the chalky mint tablet dissolved in his mouth, he spun his chair around and stared out across the river. For a moment he watched as two geese flew above the brown swirling water before swooping under the ornate arch of Lendal Bridge, then he picked up the phone. With a heavy heart he dialled the number for Jonty Woodhead, the accountant.

"Is Paul Le Vel a client of yours?" Shadow asked, after exchanging the usual greetings.

"No," replied the accountant.

"Has he ever been?"

There was a pause at the end of the line.

"Yes, when he was listed as a director of his father's company."

"Was the company wound up when Ernie Level died?"

Another pause.

"No it went into liquidation. You do know you could find all this information at Companies House don't you, Shadow?"

Shadow ignored him.

"Did Paul change his name to Le Vel after that?"

Another even longer pause.

"He was called Paul Level when he was my client."

Shadow thanked the accountant for his time once more. It seemed Le Vel hadn't always been the successful businessman he liked people to think he was. Shadow then made a call to the estate agent whose board was in the window of the old coin shop on Swinegate and made an appointment to view.

After noting down the time, he let his thoughts drift back to the whiteboards downstairs. He was certain whoever stole the coins couldn't be working alone. On the back of one of the many ignored Post-it Notes that littered his desk, he began jotting down names. Stephanie and Tim were married, but it seemed her loyalty lay with Pete. Then there was Pete and Glenn who seemed practically inseparable. Dorothy he now knew was friends with Genevieve and then he came back to Le Vel who may or may not be in a relation-ship with Jacqui. For a moment he stared at the list with arrows he'd drawn linking names, but it didn't help: he still couldn't see how it all fitted together.

He screwed up the Post-it and tossed it into the bin. Then he spent a peaceful hour completing the *Yorkshire Post* crossword. When the last clue was solved, he pulled on his jacket and left his office, avoiding both Tom and Jimmy.

SHADOW HAD ARRANGED to meet the estate agent outside Ernest Level's old shop. The young man in the shiny suit, holding his mobile phone to his ear arrived a few minutes after him. He shook Shadow's hand and unlocked the door while still continuing his conversation. Shadow stepped inside. It was cold, damp and quite dark with a musty smell. Shadow tried flicking on the light switch, but the electricity appeared to have been turned off. As the agent was still talking, he took the opportunity to take a look around unhindered. There was an old glass-topped counter and a few wooden shelves still screwed to the wall. In the back office there was nothing more than a faded green carpet covering the floor and a large safe in the corner. Shadow knelt down to take a closer look. It was bolted to the wall and floor, but the door was unlocked, and it was empty inside.

"That's available by separate negotiation I believe, Mr Shadow," said the agent, who had finally finished his call. Shadow had failed to mention he was with the police when he made the appointment.

"Can I see the upper floors?" he asked.

"Of course, no problemo. Follow me," replied the young man.

The first floor consisted of a small kitchen, an even smaller cloakroom and what must have once been the jeweller's workroom but was now empty of all equipment. The second floor looked like it had only every been used for storage with its low sloping ceilings and shelves running along the walls. Everything was covered in cobwebs and a thick layer of dust.

Shadow felt disappointed. He wasn't sure what he'd hoped to find. All he knew was that if Ling was still alive, she had to be hidden away somewhere in the city, but it was clear nobody had been in here for months. With a heavy sigh he made his way back down the stairs while the agent still chattered away behind him, extolling the virtues of being located in such a fashionable area of the city.

"What business did you say you were in?" the young man asked, when his volley of comments had failed to get a response from his client.

"I dabble in this and that," replied Shadow evasively.

"You sound like the previous owner and his son for that matter."

"Is that so?"

"Yes, Paul's a great bloke. He's got a chocolate shop over on Monk Bar Court. Does a lot of exporting, so he tells me."

"Didn't he want to use this place for his own business?"

"No, maybe he thought it was too close the other chocolatier's."

"Maybe he simply preferred Monk Bar Court."

"He can't like it that much. His lease runs out in two months and he hasn't made any plans to renew as far as I know."

Shadow paused for a moment, feeling a little confused.

"When you said previous owner, did you mean Ernest Level or Paul?"

"Well both really. Paul inherited this place from his dad. He rented it out for a few years, but then he sold it a couple of months ago to an investment company."

"I see," Shadow replied. Had he known this before, he probably wouldn't have bothered viewing the place. "Well thank you for showing me the property. I'll think about it," he said as he stepped back out into the street. The estate agent's face dropped with disappointment and he hurried out after him, but before he could press Shadow on his plans, his mobile rang again. Shadow waved goodbye to the young man as he tried to balance the phone between his ear and shoulder and lock the shop door at the same time.

Shadow had only taken a couple of steps when he almost collided with Ellie Treanor hurrying out of her own shop.

"Oh, hello there," she said, her eyes flicking over to the estate agent who was still chatting and struggling with the door. "Am I getting you as a new neighbour?" she asked.

"No, nothing like that," replied Shadow briskly. "You look like you're in a rush."

"Yes, I'm on a mission of mercy. Jacqui is desperate to finish a specially commissioned pair of earrings for a customer down in London. It seems we are both working to a tight deadline this week, but being Jacqui, she has run out of earring backs. I'm taking her some silver ones. Honestly, she's so forgetful! It wasn't a problem, of course, when she was next door."

"Perhaps she'll move back," suggested Shadow, thinking about what the agent had said regarding Le Vel not renewing his lease. Ellie's face broke into a broad smile.

"Oh that would be lovely! I know Paul convinced her she didn't need to rent somewhere so expensive when most of her business is online." Ellie paused and pursed her lips for a second. "But I do miss her. Now if you'll excuse me, I must dash. I know Jacqui wants to get the earrings finished and posted out as soon as poss!"

"Yes of course I won't keep you," he said stepping to one side as she trotted away.

"Goodbye, Chief Inspector Shadow!" she called out as she went, causing the estate agent to look round in confusion. Shadow ignored him and set off in the opposite direction. His plan for trying to visit the old coin shop incognito had failed. He should have known better than to think he wouldn't be spotted by someone who knew him. York might technically be a city but take away the tourists and students and it felt more like a small town.

The phone in his pocket buzzed. He took it out and squinted at the screen. It told him he had missed two calls from Tom and there was a text from Jimmy telling him the insurance company hadn't received a claim from the museum as yet. He returned the phone to his pocket and kept walking. While he was considering this last piece of information, he passed a newsagent's and noticed the latest edition of *The Herald* in their window. 'Mystery at the Museum' read the headline accompanied by a slightly blurred photo of Ben and Ollie in their forensic suits standing outside the Eboracum Museum.

Shadow sighed and shook his head. So much for keeping things on the QT. Tim Dunnington would not be pleased. Another visit he had failed to keep quiet.

As he left the Swinegate Quarter, he recalled he had forgotten to collect his bag of dirty laundry that needed to be dropped off at Maggie's, so he changed direction and headed towards the river. On his way back to *Florence* he picked up a pork pie from his favourite shop on Shambles to have for his lunch. Some peace and quiet on the river was exactly what he needed.

Unfortunately, peace and quiet eluded him. He had no sooner finished his last mouthful of pie than his neighbours, the geese started honking loudly. They had been sat quietly on his roof, basking in the winter sun when he arrived, but now something had clearly upset them.

"For crying out loud," he complained to himself.

As he stepped off *Florence* with the bag of laundry in his hand, he saw Dr Shepherd walking along the path towards him. She was accompanied by Pendle, the unfortunate dog from Genevieve's café.

"Isn't it a lovely afternoon, Chief Inspector?" Dorothy said as she drew closer. "Genevieve is busy at the café, so Pendle and I thought we'd make the most of it."

Shadow watched as the one-eyed, three-legged dog careered down the path, sending the furious geese honking on to the river.

"Nothing slows him down does it?" he remarked, his lips almost twitching into a smile.

"A bit like his owner." Dorothy laughed. "Genevieve doesn't let anything stop her getting what she wants either. Is there any news about the investigation at all, Chief Inspector?"

"There are a few leads we are following," Shadow replied. "I should warn you though, *The Herald* are running a story about the museum in this evening's edition. I doubt you will be able to contain news of the theft for long."

"It was only a matter of time I suppose." Dorothy sighed. "However, the world of museums is a small one and word soon spreads. Our reputation is probably already completely shot. It's going to take nothing short of a miracle to restore the Eboracum's standing in the eyes of the other curators and museum directors."

Shadow nodded sympathetically.

"I understand an insurance claim hasn't been made yet."

"No, the company has been informed of course, but as we still aren't exactly sure of what's been taken..." She trailed off and sighed. "I rather think Tim hoped you might recover the stolen pieces and the whole nasty business could be forgotten about."

Shadow diplomatically decided not to say anything, but his face must have shown what he thought of Tim Dunnington. Dr Shepherd smiled and patted him on the arm.

"Don't worry, Chief Inspector, the rest of us are a little more realistic. I know you are trying your best, but I doubt very much I shall ever see those beautiful coins again."

Shadow watched as she continued her walk along the path. He jumped slightly as she gave a surprisingly piercing whistle and Pendle bounded away from the geese to join her.

As the sun was still shining, Shadow decided to walk along the section of the city walls that led back to Lendal Bridge. He had no desire to return to the station where the atmosphere had felt strained all morning. Besides, the fresh air might help him think. His mind drifted to Le Vel and what Ellie had said about him encouraging Jacqui to leave Swinegate. Why would he encourage her to move when, at that time, she would have been paying him rent? Even Ellie, who clearly wasn't a big fan of Le Vel's, seemed to think it was a nice thing to do. Had Shadow got the man all wrong?

When he approached the river, he spotted Jake pulling a wheeled basket and throwing a stick for a delighted Missy. He paused to watch them for a moment. In his opinion, throwing a stick for a dog was one of life's simple pleasures. Jake might sleep out in the cold every night, but right now Shadow couldn't help but envy him just a little.

CHAPTER SEVEN

Down 5.

This structure stopped them all going South or West (5 letters)

"WHAT ARE YOU staring at?"

Shadow felt himself blush. He'd been studying Maggie's hands as she was writing out his receipt. He thought he was being discreet, but it obviously hadn't gone unnoticed.

"I was just looking at your hands to see if they were—" he struggled to think of the right words "—um, age-appropriate."

Maggie gave him a withering look.

"Have you never thought of opening a charm school, John?"

"Sorry, it's only because someone mentioned the missing Chinese girl's hands," he tried to explain, although he wasn't about to admit that he'd become slightly obsessed with looking at people's hands and feet. From Jacqui's scars to Le Vel's pudgy fingers and Glenn's tiny feet to Ben's massive ones.

"Well, I'm long overdue a manicure," said Maggie as she

assessed her fingernails with a frown. "The nail bar I normally go to was shut down suddenly."

"Would this be the same place Stephanie Dunnington visited?"

"That little madam! Heavens she must have been their best customer—she was never out of the place," replied Maggie. Her lips folded into a line and she raised an eyebrow. Her look told Shadow everything he needed to know about Maggie's opinion of Stephanie. "Apparently they were employing illegal immigrants there," she added. "Well I say employing; as it turns out it was more like exploiting them. Not paying the minimum wage, terrible working conditions. I used to go at least once a month. I should have noticed something wasn't right."

"Did any of the girls ever say anything to you?"

"No, I don't think they spoke much English and you know how I like to rattle on."

Shadow tried not to smile. That may have been the understatement of the year.

"Where were they from?" he asked, wondering if there could be any connection to Jing. Now, it was Maggie's turn to look embarrassed.

"I'm ashamed to say I don't for sure. Vietnam I think, but it's hard to say. They only said the odd word and they all had their long dark hair tied back and wore masks covering their mouths and noses. I should have paid more attention. I felt terrible for them when I heard about what happened.

Once when I was there, I tried asking one of the girls where her home was. I'm sure she said Ho Chi Minh City, but the only thing I knew about the place was that it used to be called Saigon. Then all I could think to tell her was how much I liked the musical, you know, *Miss Saigon*. How flippant of me to witter on about a trip to the West End when she was probably scared and lonely."

Maggie was clearly cross with herself. The writing on his receipt was becoming more and more erratic. As she spoke, Shadow suddenly remembered the girls working in Le Vel's chocolatier's kitchen with their hair covered along with the lower half of their faces. He'd been as guilty as Maggie of not paying them closer attention. He quickly looked at his watch. Chocolates from Old Elbow Lane would be closing in a few minutes.

"I'll be back soon to pick up the receipt," he said as he headed to the door.

"Where are you off to in such a hurry?" Maggie asked in surprise.

"I just need to go and check something," he called over his shoulder as he stepped out into the street.

He hurried towards Monk Bar. All the shops were closing for the evening and the Minster was striking five. As he turned into Monk Bar Court, he saw the light was still on at the chocolate shop. He opened the door and there was a jangle from the old-fashioned bell as he stepped inside. The shop itself was empty and as he looked through into the kitchen, he could see the four assistants. They were chatting to each other as they removed their old-fashioned hats and aprons and hadn't noticed him arrive. With a feeling of relief, he saw that they were three blondes and a redhead.

Shadow looked over to a door in the corner of the shop. He knew he wouldn't have another opportunity like this. Quickly he hurried over to open it and found a small stairwell with steps leading up to the first floor. He crept up them quietly, still listening to the chatter of the girls below. At the top of the stairs was a small bathroom and kitchen and an open-plan living area with a desk and sofa bed. Its layout reminded Shadow of the old coin shop, but Le Vel was nowhere to be seen. Shadow glanced around the living area. He didn't have much time. The girls would be leaving and locking up any minute and he didn't want to be shut in here all night or, worse still, be found by Le Vel. There was a desk with a computer, a filing cabinet—nothing out of the ordinary. Then he noticed in the corner of the ceiling a loft hatch. There was a pole resting in the corner with a metal hook. It was obviously there to open the hatch.

Below the girls were still laughing and joking. He reached for the pole, raised it and flicked the metal catch then quickly stepped back and the hatch dropped, and a metal ladder rattled down. Shadow held his breath. It had made quite a noise. The girls below were now silent. Quickly he climbed the metal steps and stuck his head into the loft. There was a light switch to his left. He flicked it on. The loft was empty. Clean and tidy, but empty. He'd been convinced he would find something, but he was wrong. He flicked off the light, climbed down the ladder and closed the hatch again just in time. There was a sound behind him and the redhead and one of the blonde girls arrived at the doorway looking nervous and armed with an umbrella and a small toffee hammer.

"Hello there," Shadow said calmly with what he hoped was a reassuring smile. "I was looking for Mr Le Vel. Is he not here?"

"No, I'm sorry he's gone to visit a customer in Leeds," the redhead explained, glancing at her colleague. Neither looked entirely convinced by Shadow's explanation.

"Oh well, I'll catch up with him later," replied Shadow easily and he followed the girls downstairs and outside on to the cobbles. He watched as the redhead locked up. She gave him a sidelong look as she wished him a good night. At the same time, Jacqui Heaton was also locking up her shop.

"Oh, hello, Chief Inspector. What are you doing here? Was Paul expecting you? Is there anything I can help you with?"

"Yes actually there is, Miss Heaton," he replied as he recalled something that had been bothering him since he spoke to Ellie Treanor. "I believe you used to rent the shop on Swinegate that once belong to Ernest Level."

"That's right," she replied, then blushed. "That's how I first met Paul. He'd inherited the building, so briefly he was my landlord, but only for about six months; then he convinced me to move here."

"Why did he do that do you think?"

"Well I suppose he thought it would be nice for us to work close together," she said with a self-conscious smile. "It was much more economical, I don't mind telling you, but that's Paul all over. He's always thinking of others—so considerate," she gushed, then added, "Also, he wanted to sell the place on Swinegate. Maybe he thought it was better for it to be empty."

Shadow nodded, but privately he thought the investment company would have preferred to buy the place with a sitting tenant.

"When you were in the Swinegate shop, I don't suppose you can remember if Ernest, Paul's father, had left any of his old equipment behind?" he asked.

"No, Paul had cleared the place out before I moved in. He said it was full of all sorts of old junk his dad had hoarded over the years."

"I see. Well thank you for your time, Miss Heaton. Have a good evening."

AS HE LEFT Monk Bar Court and stepped on to Goodramgate, a loud sing-songy voice called out to him from above.

"Yoo-hoo! Chief Inspector Shadow!"

Shadow looked up to see Genevieve Knott poking her head out and waving at him from one of the windows in the café.

"May I borrow you for a moment? I need your assistance urgently."

Reluctantly, Shadow nodded and trudged up the narrow stairs, inwardly cursing Jimmy for getting him involved with Miss Knott. She was waiting for him in the café doorway.

"Ah there you are!" she exclaimed needlessly.

"Is there a problem, Miss Knott?"

"Indeed there is, Chief Inspector. Now you come inside and I'll get you a nice cup of lapsang souchong and tell you all about it."

Shadow resigned himself to the fact that the next ten minutes of his day would be totally wasted as he sat down at the table nearest the door. There was a noticeboard on the wall next to him covered in leaflets for various worthy causes. Genevieve promptly returned carrying a cup and saucer and brandishing what looked like a bill.

"What do you make of this, Chief Inspector?" she asked, slapping the piece of paper on to the table in front him as she plonked herself down in the seat opposite. Shadow fished his reading glasses out of his jacket pocket, placed them on his nose and peered at the sheet in front of him. His guess had been correct. It was a bill. An electric bill for the last quarter and quite a high one. He looked up, still puzzled.

"I'm sorry, Miss Knott, but I don't quite understand

what this has to do with me."

"Look at the figure, Chief Inspector, look how high it is. It's more than double the amount I paid last quarter."

"I'm still not clear what you want me to do," replied Shadow, making a mental note to check with George and see if there was history of insanity in the Knott family. Genevieve's eyes opened wide behind the thick lenses of her glasses.

"Well I telephoned the electricity company and the silly girl I spoke to couldn't explain why. It's a mystery! So, I thought to myself: Genevieve, who could solve this mystery for you. I looked down into the street and there you were. A detective to solve my mystery!"

Shadow shifted uncomfortably in his chair as Genevieve beamed at him.

"It's crimes I tend to solve rather than mysteries, Miss Knott," he attempted to explain patiently, but she quickly interrupted him.

"It is a crime, Chief Inspector! Daylight robbery! I shall leave it in your capable hands. You can keep that copy; I made it for you. I know you won't let me down."

With that she stood up and swooped on a couple of unsuspecting tourists who had arrived, leaving Shadow alone with the enormous electric bill. Wearily he folded it into his pocket as he stood up to make his escape, but before he left a thought struck him. Who was working upstairs in the kitchen? While Genevieve was practising her Chinese on the new arrivals, Shadow edged past and ducked behind the counter and up the rickety wooden stairs in the corner. They led him straight into the kitchen. Despite the ancient room it was housed in, all the equipment and work surfaces were in modern stainless steel. However, what Shadow noticed first were the five familiar figures already in the room. Darren and Jared Clarkson were twin brothers, who the last time he'd seen them were being sentenced to two years in a young offenders' institute. The pair of them had been completely out of control. For six months they'd been responsible for a reign of chaos in the city. Barely a day went by when one or both of them weren't arrested for shoplifting or being drunk and disorderly.

Shadow was amazed. He didn't know they'd been released. The third figure was Jake. He was perched on the deep stone windowsill, a cigarette in his hand as always. Finally, and mercifully asleep, were Pendle and Missy, curled up together on a large fluffy cushion in the corner.

"Gone into the catering business have we, gentlemen?" Shadow asked the Clarkson twins. Darren and Jared looked up from chopping vegetables and exchanged a wary glance.

"We got a certificate in food preparation while we was inside," replied Darren defensively.

Shadow raised a sceptical eyebrow as he wondered whose idea it had been to encourage the pair of delinquents to use knives.

"Gen took us on when we got out," added Jared. "Our

parole officer told us about her. She gave us a chance when nobody else wanted to know. He told her we'd found God."

"I'd no idea he was missing," muttered Shadow. He turned to Jake. "What about you? Do you fancy yourself as the next Gordon Ramsay too?" he asked.

Jake almost smiled as he blew a plume of smoke out of the window.

"We met Gen and Pendle down by the river a couple of days ago. She offered me a job here, but I couldn't be cooped up inside all day. She said I could deliver the lunch orders to all the offices instead. I get twenty quid for doing it, the hostel on Micklegate charges fifteen, so we get to stay somewhere warm every night."

Shadow nodded. That explained the basket he'd seen Jake with down by the river.

"It sounds like the perfect arrangement," he replied. Jake glanced across to his sleeping dog, took a last drag and stubbed out the cigarette on the stone.

"It'll get us through winter."

Satisfied that Ling wasn't on the premises, Shadow made his way back down to the seating area of the café. He still had no idea how the place could function profitably, but at least it wasn't harbouring illegal migrants. At the bottom of the stairs he almost bumped into Genevieve, who was laden down with empty plates. She looked surprised to see him there.

"I didn't know you were still here, Chief Inspector," she

said.

"I thought I should have a quick look at the kitchen," said Shadow, hoping his explanation didn't sound too vague, but Genevieve looked delighted.

"Jolly good! On the case already. I knew I could rely on you. Did you find anything amiss up there?" she asked eagerly.

"No, not yet, Miss Knott," he replied as he retreated out of the café and down the steps of the gatehouse. Actually, he suspected two snoring dogs and someone smoking a cigarette in a commercial kitchen was probably more than amiss when it came to breaking hygiene regulations. No doubt had he mentioned this to Genevieve, she would tell him rules were there to be broken. Perhaps she was right; it was after all what kept him employed.

BACK DOWN ON Goodramgate, Maggie was still waiting for him in the laundry, drumming her fingers on the counter.

"You took your time. I should have closed thirty minutes ago."

"I know. I'm sorry. It's been an eventful half hour. I got collared by Genevieve Knott. That woman is impossible to say no to."

"Really, not like poor Julie then?" she asked, giving him a quizzical look.

"What? The waitress from Bettys?" Shadow asked. He'd forgotten all about her.

"Yes, she got sick of waiting for you to make a move and decided to leave with one of the pastry chefs instead. They're opening a café in Helmsley together."

Shadow's brow furrowed. He'd wondered why he hadn't seen his usual waitress for a while. Then he noticed Maggie was grinning at him. Sometimes it was impossible to know if she was teasing him or not.

"Well if she has left, I can't see what it has to do with me. As usual you are listening to gossip and letting your imagination run away with you," he replied defensively. "You'll be saying there's something going on between me and Miss Knott next."

"You are not her type in any way, shape or form." Maggie cackled, irritating Shadow even more.

"I forgot you're the expert when it come to the private lives of York's residents," he snapped.

Maggie folded her arms and narrowed her eyes. Never a good sign.

"John, Genevieve is in a relationship with Dorothy Shepherd and has been for ages."

"Dr Shepherd from the Eboracum Museum?"

"Yes, they're both Quakers. They met when Dorothy first moved to York and began attending the same meeting house as Genevieve—you know the one down on Friargate."

As if to prove Maggie's point Dr Shepherd hurried by

the window. They both watched as she entered the door in the gatehouse that led up to Genevieve's café. Suddenly seeing her walking Pendle and visiting Camilla Dunnington with Genevieve made a lot more sense. However, did it mean anything with regard to the missing coins? Shadow wondered, but Maggie hadn't finished.

"And as for implying that I'm nosy," she continued, her tone becoming more combative with every word, "I'm not the only one. You notice what people are doing just as much as I do. It's just that I'm better at communicating what I see, but that doesn't make me a gossip."

"Whatever you say, Maggie," Shadow replied with a weary sigh. He picked up his receipt. It was pointless to argue that his job required him to be interested in other people. Whatever he said, Maggie was bound to have the last word. She could be quite impossible at times.

HE LEFT THE laundry in a foul mood and walked along Goodramgate with his head down, staring at the pavement. He couldn't shake the feeling of irritation talking to Maggie had given him. Perhaps it was because they'd known each other since they were children, but she had a habit of making him think about things he would rather ignore. It was disconcerting to say the least. He would never admit it, but he'd had an inkling that Julie had been interested in being more than friends, ever since she'd paid a visit to *Florence* when he'd injured his ankle, but he had tried to ignore the situation. It had made him feel awkward and a little guilty. As far as he was aware, he had done nothing to encourage her and was relieved to hear she'd found somebody else.

As for being nosy, he still maintained he was simply professionally inquisitive, but maybe he shouldn't have been so grumpy with Maggie. After all, gossip or not, the information about Dorothy and Genevieve could turn out to be useful.

As he trudged along, he heard the familiar sound of trainer-clad feet jogging up behind him. A few seconds later, Jimmy arrived by his side.

"Anything new?" Shadow asked by way of a greeting.

"Not really, Chief. The couple who ran the nail bar are still in custody awaiting trial, so we know they aren't involved with Ling's disappearance. Incidentally, all the girls there were Vietnamese. I've just been to the Monk Bar Hotel to speak to Mrs Chen, the tour guide and the rest of the party before for they leave for Edinburgh. None of them have heard from or seen Ling while they've been in the city. The tour guide did say something interesting though." But before Jimmy could continue there was a strong gust of wind and the heavens opened. Suddenly hailstones started raining down like tiny freezing bullets, bouncing off the pavement and hitting the two detectives in the face. Shadow flinched and silently pointed to The Cross Keys on the other side of the road and the two of them put their heads down and dashed over and through the door.

Wiping the hail from his hair and jacket, Shadow went to the bar while Jimmy—who was shaking himself like a soaked spaniel—found them a table by the roaring open fire. A few moments later, Shadow returned with a pint for himself and a mineral water for his sergeant. He placed their drinks on the table and shrugged off his still-dripping jacket before taking a seat.

"Go on then what did the tour guide have to say?"

"Only that he contacted the head office at the tour company to tell them that one of his party had gone missing, but they said they had no record of Ling Li booking a place. The ticket she showed him must have been a fake."

Shadow frowned as he took a sip of beer and thought for a moment.

"A more experienced guide might have been able to spot a fake or know to check with head office before letting someone join the tour."

"When I questioned the guide, he said he thought it was strange, but felt sorry for Ling. She said she had hitchhiked to the service station in a van and the guide said he didn't think he should leave a young girl behind. He could of course be covering for himself. Do you think he's involved somehow?"

"No, not necessarily, but it still doesn't make sense. How would she know where the coach would be and how would a girl who doesn't speak much English convince someone to give her a lift? Somebody she knew must have driven her there."

"It's been well over forty-eight hours since she was seen in York. She could be anywhere in the country by now. Do you think we should go to the national media?"

"Maybe but I get the feeling that getting her to York was carefully planned. I think she's still here; we just need to find out where and why." He took another sip of his pint while he thought.

"Oh, by the way, Chief, Tom showed the list of museum volunteers to George, but he didn't think any of them were related to Paul Le Vel or his father."

Shadow sighed. It had been too much hope there might have been a connection there.

"I had a look around Le Vel's place earlier. I thought there was a chance I might find something," he said.

For once Jimmy, didn't respond, but he looked uncomfortable as he sipped his mineral water.

"You really don't think he's involved?" asked Shadow.

Jimmy twiddled with the edge of his beer mat for a few seconds before looking his boss in the eye. "Honestly, Chief, I think you might be letting the fact you don't like Le Vel cloud your judgement. You could get into a lot of trouble going in there without his permission or a search warrant and if you really want me to be honest, I don't think the magistrates would grant you a warrant simply because Paul's father used to deal in old coins and he's been to China a few times. This time I really do think it is just a coincidence."

Shadow was stunned for a moment. It was the first time his sergeant had ever directly criticised a decision he'd made and deep down he knew he was right about the search warrant. Entering the chocolate shop flat without permission had been foolish. He had never been the sort of police officer who liked to the bend the rules, not least because following the proper procedures meant the case was less vulnerable to being torn apart by some clever barrister when it got to court. However, on this occasion he'd behaved recklessly. The thought of Ling being in the city and needing their help bothered him more than many of the murder investigations he'd worked on. He'd taken a chance at Le Vel's because he was sure he would find something to help them locate the missing girl, but he'd been wrong.

"It was only a quick look. I was in and out in less than five minutes," he said sounding overly defensive even to himself. They sat in awkward silence for a while, sipping their drinks. Jimmy continued to fiddle with his beer mat and Shadow stared out of the window. It was true he didn't like Le Vel, but there were plenty of people he didn't like and he didn't think they were all capable of being criminals. He downed the last of his pint.

"Come on, the hail has stopped. Let's make a move."

The moment the two detectives stood up to leave, Paul Le Vel walked through the door. He smiled broadly when he saw them and came straight over.

"Chief Inspector, Sergeant Chang, good to see you both. Can I buy you a drink or is that not allowed when you are on duty?" he asked pleasantly.

"Thank you, Mr Le Vel, but we were just leaving," replied Shadow.

"That's a shame, Chief Inspector, I heard you were looking for me earlier."

"Yes, I called in at the chocolate shop, but you weren't there."

"Well I'm sorry I missed you. You feel free to pop by any time now, no need for a warrant or anything. We've nothing to hide at Monk Bar Court."

WHEN THEY WERE out in the street, Jimmy breathed a loud sigh of relief.

"Well that could have been a lot worse. He could have threatened to put in a complaint against you, Chief, but he was really understanding. I think you've got him all wrong. He seems like a nice, genuine guy."

Shadow remained unconvinced. He was sure their meeting with Le Vel wasn't a coincidence. The man wanted to let him know that he'd heard about him searching his premises without permission. Jacqui or one of the girls who worked for him must have told him. Maybe he also knew he'd been to view his father's old coin shop.

THE TWO DETECTIVES walked back to the station. Shadow was deep in thought and for once Jimmy had nothing to say either. When they arrived, they found an agitated-looking Tom waiting for them at the reception desk.

"Chief Inspector, Sergeant Chang, I was about to call you. A body has been found, sir."

Shadow's heart sank. They were too late. Ling wasn't hidden away anywhere. He had been fixating on Le Vel and the possible connection to the stolen coins when he should have concentrated on looking for the lost girl.

"Where?" he asked.

"That's why I was coming to look for you in particular, sir. It's at Mrs Jackson's house." The young constable paused and looked embarrassed. "I know she's a friend of yours."

Shadow suddenly felt as if all the air had been sucked out of his lungs. He put his hand out on the desk to steady himself. He'd been speaking to her only an hour ago and they hadn't parted on good terms. He felt Jimmy place a hand on his shoulder.

"Has the body been identified, Tom? Is it Mrs Jackson?" Shadow heard his sergeant ask.

"No it was Mrs Jackson who made the call. I don't know the identity, but I think Sophie is already there."

A wave of relief swept over Shadow.

"A word of advice, Constable," he snapped. "If you want your career to progress, I suggest you work on how you break the news of a body being found during a missing persons investigation." And with that he headed back out of the door. He then had to wait for what felt like an eternity in the station car park as Jimmy located an available vehicle to take them to Maggie's. Silently he paced up and down, shocked at how distraught he'd been by the thought that something had happened to her.

MAGGIE LIVED IN a small cottage opposite Clifton Green about a mile away from the city centre. Jimmy drove them there through the rush hour traffic and for once Shadow didn't grumble about his sergeant's speed. As they arrived in Clifton, they saw Sophie standing by her own car. It looked like she was preparing to leave.

"What have we got?" asked Shadow abruptly.

Sophie gave him a reassuring smile. "Don't worry, Chief, it's not one for us. We're about two thousand years too late. Maggie is fine and the archaeologists are in there now."

"Stather?" asked Jimmy as Shadow breathed a huge sigh of relief.

"No, he's on holiday staying with Donaldson at his villa in Portugal, would you believe?" Sophie said with a grin.

Shadow raised an eyebrow. He shouldn't really be surprised the two men were friends. It was hard to say which of them was the more pompous.

"Isn't he supposed to be checking the rest of the Roman coins?" asked Jimmy.

"I guess he thought playing golf with Donaldson was more important," Sophie replied. "I heard the chief constable is out there too."

"Huh, the holy trinity is complete," snorted Shadow. At least now he knew why he hadn't been harangued for calling out the dive team yet. "If Stather's away, who did you phone instead?" he asked.

"Dr Shepherd—she always deputises for Stather when he's away," Sophie explained as she loaded her bag back into the car and closed the boot with a slam.

Shadow left Sophie talking to Jimmy and hurried through the gate and round to the back garden. Floodlights were already glaring at the ground and a tent was being erected over the area where the builders must have been digging the foundations for Maggie's extension. Dr Shepherd and two assistants were standing in the trench. Dorothy looked positively animated beneath the bright lights.

"Such exciting news, Chief Inspector. This could be it. What we've been looking for. We might actually be close to finding the site of York's own amphitheatre."

"Why do you think that?" he asked, peering down at the skeleton that was still half covered in mud.

"This first body has clearly been beheaded and there's a second skeleton here too with marks on the bones consistent with injuries from the claws of a lion or something similar. I know I shouldn't get carried away—I've only been here ten minutes—but looking at the size of the skeletons, I think they could be slaves who hailed from North Africa. It's quite possible these were gladiators."

For the second time that week, Shadow thought how little humans had changed over the centuries. These days people may think they were more civilised than the barbaric Romans, but they were still bringing others away from their homeland and exploiting them for financial gain. Only now modern slaves were put to work in sweatshops rather than being made to fight in arenas. As he pondered this Dr Shepherd was still talking.

"One of the archaeology students who came to assist me has already discovered a small token bearing the image of the goddess Minerva. If this is the gladiator's burial ground then the amphitheatre can't have been far from here. It's incredible—only today I told you the Eboracum Museum needed a miracle. Well, this could be it!"

Despite Dr Shepherd's excitement, Shadow was now only half listening. He had noticed Maggie through the kitchen window. She looked pale as she sat at the table, her hands wrapped around a mug. He excused himself from the archaeologists and knocked gently on the back door before stepping inside. Maggie looked up and gave him a weak smile.

"Sorry, John. I called the police in a panic. I got a taxi home after you'd gone because it was pouring down. As I ran in, I happened to look in the trench and saw that horrible bony hand sticking out, but it turned out to be nothing for you, I'm afraid. Now I feel like a prize fool."

"It doesn't matter about that. Are you all right?"

"Just a bit shaken up and heaven knows when I'll get my extension finished now. One of the young archaeologists said they could out there for weeks."

Shadow knew she was trying to make light of the situation, but he could still hear the tremor in her voice.

"I'll make you a cup of tea, Mrs Jackson," offered Jimmy who had followed Shadow inside without him noticing.

"Thanks, love, but Sophie made me one, bless her. She said I looked like I was in shock. Now if you'll both excuse me, I'm going to throw a few things into a bag. I can't stay here tonight."

For a second Shadow considered inviting her to stay on *Florence*, but before he could say anything Jimmy spoke instead.

"I don't blame you. Where will you go?"

"I'm going to stay in the flat above the laundry. Sam used to live there. The bedroom is still full of all his old junk, but at least I won't have to wake up to a garden full of skeletons. I won't sleep a wink if I stay here."

"We can give you a lift if you like; can't we, Chief?" offered Jimmy.

"Yes, of course, whenever you are ready," agreed Shadow.

"You are both very kind," she said as she left the room still clutching her mug of tea. Shadow looked around him. He'd never visited Maggie's home before, but if he'd had to picture it, it would have looked exactly like this: cosy and cluttered with a beamed ceiling so low, Jimmy couldn't stand up straight. The walls were painted bright yellow, pots of herbs filled the windowsill, a pile of well-thumbed cookery books were piled next to the cooker and the fridge was covered in photos, postcards, invitations and clippings from magazines and newspapers. It was about as far removed from Shadow and his starkly furnished home as one could imagine.

He wandered over to the CD collection stacked on the worktop next to an old stereo. He nodded in approval at the titles. All the greats were there: Louis Armstrong, Billie Holiday, Duke Ellington.

As a schoolboy he had occasionally visited Maggie's family home. He had always been slightly stunned by the loud, chaotic atmosphere there compared to the sombre house he shared with his mother. Maggie's house was always full of noise and people, and her mother, a small Irishwoman with the same laughing eyes as Maggie, reigned supreme. She was bossy and funny and seemed capable of carrying on several conversations at once. By contrast, Maggie's father was a quiet, gentle giant of a man, who usually sat in the corner of the room nodding good-naturedly as his wife fired off orders, instructions and reprimands to their brood. He was a trumpet player in a band and had let the ten-year-old Maggie and Shadow sneak into the smoke-filled club on Micklegate where he played. That's when Shadow had first fallen in love with jazz music.

MAGGIE REAPPEARED A few moments later dragging a bulging holdall behind her. Jimmy hauled it on to his shoulders and carried it to the car for her, as Shadow took her arm and escorted her past the archaeologists who were still working beneath the floodlights. He felt her give a slight shudder as they passed the hole containing the skeletons.

"For heaven's sake don't put any flashing lights or sirens on will you? The neighbours probably already have me down as a mass murderer," she said as she slid into the back seat of the car.

Shadow smiled to himself as he closed the door. At least she hadn't lost her sense of humour. Just then there was a flash of light behind them. Shadow turned, slightly dazed, to find Kevin MacNab and a photographer standing there with him. The journalist immediately launched a barrage of questions at him.

"Do you have a quote for our readers, Chief Inspector Shadow? I hear a body has been found. Is it the missing

Chinese girl? Is Mrs Jackson under arrest?"

"No she is not," growled Shadow, "and if any photographs of Mrs Jackson or her house appear in your rag, I'll have you both charged with invasion of privacy."

THE FLAT ABOVE Maggie's laundry was spread over two floors. The top floor had a bedroom and bathroom with low sloping ceilings and the first floor had a small kitchen and sitting room. It was clean and cosy and despite what Maggie had said, there were only a few cardboard boxes taped up and labelled 'Sam', belonging to Maggie's son who now lived in Alicante with his Spanish girlfriend.

The walls were painted a warm shade of cream and there was a thick oatmeal-coloured carpet covering the living room floor. The sitting room was sparsely furnished with a sofa and a small pine table and chairs. The only items that looked out of place were the huge posters of Messi, Ronaldo and other European footballers stuck on the walls.

"Are you a football fan, Mrs Jackson?" asked Jimmy as he placed the heavy bag down on the floor with a thud. Maggie grinned and shook her head.

"No, but Sam is. He lived up here before he decided he'd rather run a bar in the sun than down Walmgate," she said, "although sometimes I think he only moved over there to be able to watch his beloved Barcelona play."

Shadow peered into the kitchen while she was talking. It looked even less well stocked than the galley in *Florence*. He cleared his throat.

"There isn't much to eat in here. Would you like to go to Catania's for dinner?"

Maggie and Jimmy turned to look at him in surprise. They both knew he usually preferred to dine alone; in fact, he almost had an aversion to eating with others. Under their gaze, Shadow shrugged his shoulders awkwardly.

"Or I could get you a takeaway?"

"That's kind, John," replied Maggie with a gentle smile, "but after seeing those skeletons I really don't have much of an appetite. There's some milk and biscuits downstairs in the laundry fridge, if I get peckish later."

Shadow nodded and cleared his throat again, feeling a mixture of relief and embarrassment.

"Well that's all right then, good, excellent. We'll leave you in peace, shall we? Come along, Sergeant," he said already halfway down the stairs.

"Goodbye and thank you!" Maggie called after him.

LATER THAT EVENING, after eating another hurried meal at Catania's, Shadow walked home along the river. His breath formed clouds in the cold night air as he mulled over the day's events. Above him the clear night sky was full of stars shining like pinpricks of light through a moth-eaten blanket. *There'll be a frost tonight*, he thought as he stepped aboard *Florence*. Inside, he couldn't help comparing the sparse interior of his home to Maggie's cottage. Even the flat she was staying in had seemed cosier than his home. Aside from his books and CDs there was little to show he had lived there for twenty-five years. For the short time Luisa had lived there too, the place had been filled with brightly coloured cushions and throws and a vase full of flowers always on the table. Perhaps he should make an effort and buy some pictures for the walls or a few house plants, he thought to himself as he flopped into bed.

THE NEXT MORNING, his prediction of a hard frost was proved right. When he stepped on to the towpath the sun was shining and it looked like the city had been dusted in icing sugar. He turned up the collar of his old wax jacket and set off at a brisk pace. He'd almost reached Skeldergate Bridge when two familiar figures came into view.

"There you are, Chief! We were just on our way to come and find you," said Jimmy sounding slightly muffled beneath the scarf that was covering half his face.

"Why? What's happened now?"

"Mrs Jackson has found another body, sir," replied Tom, barely able to contain himself.

"If this is your idea of a joke, Constable, it's in very poor taste," snapped Shadow.

"No, Chief, it's true. Maggie found a body this morning. It's Jacqui Heaton. Maggie found her at the bottom of the city walls," explained Jimmy.

"Where is she now?"

Jimmy and Tom both looked puzzled as they glanced at each other.

"Jacqui or Maggie, Chief?" enquired Jimmy.

"For crying out loud!" muttered Shadow and continued to curse under his breath as he marched on to the bridge and towards the city centre.

MAGGIE WAS IN her office at the back of the laundry. A young female PC was beside her and her two assistants Karen and Roz were fussing over her with cups of tea and a plate of Danish pastries. The three of them diplomatically left the room when Shadow arrived.

"This is getting to be a habit," he said, relieved to see she didn't appear to be too shaken. She gave him a wry smile.

"I'm jinxed that's what. It's a sign. I shouldn't have stayed here this February. I should have gone to visit Sam as usual. As soon as I've been to Rose's Chinese New Year celebration, I'm catching the first flight out to Spain. A bit of sun and sangria should help cheer me up."

"You're going to Rose's?" he asked, thinking it was a good sign that she still felt like socialising.

"Yes, aren't you?"

Shadow shifted uncomfortably. "It's not really my thing. Parties."

"Well you can't not go or make up an excuse. You'll look rude and Rose will be offended."

Shadow raised his eyes to the ceiling. He'd come to investigate a possible crime, not to be scolded.

"Do you think we could forget about my social engagements for a moment and concentrate on what happened this morning?" he asked.

"All right, but I've already told that nice PC everything. I had a rotten night's sleep and was up and about by the time the Minster was striking five. I realised I'd left some of my make-up and a few other bits and bobs I wanted at home. I set off down Lord Mayor's Walk. It was still dark, but the floodlights along the walls were on. I happened to glance over and saw something red. There had been a heavy frost, so it really stood out. I walked through the grass—it's quite long there—and that's when I found her. It was those red shoes of hers that caught my eye. Poor woman! She must have been there for hours, all alone. She was just lying there all crumpled and she was always so full of life."

Maggie's voice caught in her throat and Shadow instinctively put a hand on her shoulder, but she shook it off.

"It's all right. I'm fine. You go and do your job. Find out what happened to her."

CHAPTER EIGHT

Across 8.
Using legs and gum you cannot legally get across the border (7 letters)

ONLY SLIGHTLY REASSURED that Maggie was indeed all right, Shadow went to join Jimmy and the others who were by now on the city walls. He read the sign attached to the wooden door at the bottom of the stairs stating that the walls were open between 8am and dusk and closed in bad weather. At this time of year dusk was around 5pm. If Jacqui had been on the walls before then, surely she would have been discovered before Maggie found her nearly twelve hours later. He passed the entrance to Genevieve's café at the top of the stairs. It was still closed and mercifully there was no sign of the owner.

Jimmy was standing on the stretch of wall that ran alongside the shops of Monk Court. He was talking to the man responsible for opening the city walls, who confirmed that as always, he'd checked that everyone was down before locking up, shortly after five o'clock.

A little further along, Ben and Ollie from forensics were

examining a gap in the wall. Ben was holding a tape measure while Ollie was standing on his tiptoes.

"What on earth are you doing?" Shadow asked.

"If I stand on my toes, I'm the same height as the deceased," explained Ollie, "so we were doing some calculations to work out if she could have fallen or was definitely pushed."

"We think this is where she went over, Chief," said Ben as he showed Shadow an evidence bag containing a scrap of purple fabric. Shadow peered over the wall. A screen had been erected around the body and Sophie was already down there. She looked up and waved to him.

"I'll be up in a minute, Chief," she called. Shadow gave her a thumbs up and turned his attention back to the forensics team.

"So, following these calculations of yours, do we have any idea if she jumped, fell or was pushed? Any signs of a struggle?"

Both scientists wrinkled their foreheads as they considered the question.

"It's hard to say for definite without knowing her weight and exact measurements between her joints. My knees are above this lower part of the wall, but hers might not have been," pondered Ollie as he scratched his head. "Sophie said she'd fill in the blanks for us, so to speak."

"It went down to minus two last night. She could have slipped if it was icy," offered Ben, bending down to look at the slightly damp stone path.

"And it's for these deep scientific insights that we call you out." Shadow sighed.

At that moment Jimmy came to join them.

"I've spoken to the builders from the council who are working on the last two shops, Chief. They arrived to collect some tools they left here," he said pointing to the last shop in the row, which still had part of its roof missing. "I told them they'd have to come back later. They said they left at about four o'clock yesterday afternoon and Jacqui was still in her shop when they went."

"Okay," said Shadow. "Anything else?"

"Nobody is at the chocolatier's yet, but the sign on the door says they don't open until ten," replied Jimmy.

As his sergeant was talking, Shadow noticed a planning permission notice attached to the back of one of the buildings. It was Mr Wang's tea shop. The notice was regarding converting the attic of the property into a café. There was a large window that looked out on to the walls.

"It says here that Mr Wang wants to make this window a doorway," read Shadow.

"That's right, Chief," agreed Jimmy. "It's Lucy's idea. She thinks it'll be quirky to turn the attic into part of the tea shop and they'll attract tourists who are walking the walls. She's convinced her dad they should start selling bubble tea too."

For now, Shadow resisted the temptation to enquire as to

why Jimmy was so well informed about the Wangs' business plans or what on earth bubble tea was. Instead he walked further along until he was parallel with the next two buildings: Le Vel's chocolate shop and Jacqui's place. They were almost identical in design to Mr Wang's property except where there should be a window on to the walls both were boarded up with heavy wooden shutters. Shadow pointed to the ones covering Jacqui's window.

"Maybe that's how she got out here," he said. Jimmy bent down to have a closer look.

"I think you're right, Chief. It looks like they've been opened recently." He pushed against them. "But they're locked now."

Shadow looked over to Ben and Ollie, who were still fiddling with their tape measure.

"You two see if you can find something to get them open," ordered Shadow as Sophie appeared on the walls.

"Morning, Sophie!"

"Morning, Chief. Hi, Jimmy; hi, guys." She waved at Ben and Ollie before turning her attention back to Shadow and Jimmy. "By the way there's a Miss Treanor down by the gate. She seemed a bit upset and said she wanted to speak to someone."

"I'll go," said Jimmy very quickly before heading down the steps. Was it Shadow's imagination or did his sergeant seem worried and distracted? He certainly had been behaving very strangely recently, but right now Shadow had more pressing matters to deal with.

"So, what can you tell me, Sophie?" he asked.

"She died of a broken neck, almost instantly I'd say. Probably around nine or ten last night."

"Any signs of violence?"

"It's hard to be a hundred per cent. All her fingernails are all intact, there are a few cuts to her face and a graze on one hand, but she could have got those as she fell."

"Did she have her handbag with her or any keys in her pockets? It might save us trying to break into her place."

"No, sorry, nothing—not a phone or any cash."

"Had she been drinking? Taken any drugs?"

"I don't think so, but I won't know for certain until I do the post-mortem. I'll get the results to you after lunch."

"That's great thank you, Sophie."

The doctor left them, and Shadow turned to see Ben and Ollie had managed to locate a crowbar amongst the tools the builders had left behind, but they were now looking at it in confusion.

"Which end do we use?" asked Ben scratching his head.

"For crying out loud," muttered Shadow as he took hold of the metal bar, wedged it between the shutters and applied as much force as he could muster. There was a loud splintering sound and the wood gave way. Ben and Ollie started clapping and Shadow shook his head in despair.

"Don't just stand there, help remove this wood," he said as he pulled away a large chunk and peered into the attic.

From what he could see it looked similar to the one he had searched at Le Vel's place next door. At that moment, Jimmy returned.

"What did Miss Treanor want?" asked Shadow.

"I had to tell her about Jacqui, Chief. She was pretty upset. Apparently, they'd met for drinks at The Botanist last night. Jacqui realised she'd left her phone behind in her studio. She came back to get it and Ellie never saw her again. She tried calling, but there was no answer. She waited for about an hour then went home. First thing this morning, she called round to Jacqui's flat, but of course there was no response, so she came here."

"What time did Jacqui leave The Botanist?"

"About 8.30pm."

"Well that would fit in with the time of death Sophie gave us," said Shadow. He paused for a moment. "Sophie said Jacqui didn't have her phone or keys on her and these shutters were locked from the inside. That means she either didn't get on to the walls from her premises, or somebody was with her and locked the window afterwards, or possibly she died somewhere completely different and her body was moved here to make it look like she'd fallen."

Shadow turned back to the now fully exposed window opening. It was large enough for him to climb inside. The room was empty, but there was a mixture of smells that seemed familiar, but he couldn't quite place.

"What do you think, Chief?" asked Ollie who had stuck

his head in through the opening. Shadow scowled.

"I think you two should make yourselves useful and see what you can find in here."

Obediently Ben and Ollie climbed in through the window, followed by Jimmy. The room looked like it had been cleaned recently. There was no dust on the bare floorboards, but Shadow noticed a couple of round dark marks. A burn perhaps, like someone had put down a hot saucepan.

"Have a look at these," he said to Ollie as he walked over to a trapdoor in the corner. It was the same as the one in Le Vel's place. He tried to lift it open, but it was locked on the other side. He peered down and looked more closely. There seemed to be scratch marks on the door.

"Chief, I've found something," called out Ben who was examining the floorboards in the far corner of the room.

"Am I meant to guess what exactly?" enquired Shadow impatiently as he made his way over to the scientist. Ben held up a pair of his tweezers. Clamped between the blades was a very long black hair.

"Jacqui had dark hair, but it's too long to be one of hers," Shadow mused.

"I need to test it in the lab, but I don't think it belonged to anyone Caucasian, Chief."

"Could Lucy have been in here?" Shadow wondered.

"It's too long for Lucy too. Her hair is only shoulder-length," said Jimmy. Just then Lucy herself appeared in the window carrying a tray of drinks.

"I thought you might all be thirsty, so I've brought you some drinks. I'll leave the tray here."

She disappeared again to a chorus of thanks from Jimmy, Ben and Ollie, but Shadow was frowning.

"What happened to securing the crime scene? And how did she get up here?" he hissed.

"It's only Lucy, Chief, and she probably climbed out through her own attic window," replied Jimmy who had gone to retrieve the tray that held four glasses containing different pastel-coloured liquids—pink, blue, green and yellow—with a thick drinking straw in each.

"What on earth are those anyway? Milkshakes?" he asked.

"No, it's bubble tea," explained Jimmy as he handed the glasses around. "It was invented in Taiwan. Lucy learnt how to make it when she was out there."

Shadow sniffed his suspiciously. "What are the black bits floating around at the bottom?" he asked.

"Tapioca balls."

Shadow pulled a face and handed his glass back. He'd had enough of trying exotic foodstuffs and beverages for one week.

"No thank you. I'm going to leave you to it gentlemen and see if I can find Le Vel. He's been rather noticeable in his absence this morning. Let me know if you find anything else here and get through the loft hatch and into the rest of the building. See what's in Jacqui's shop and studio."

Shadow stepped back out on to the city walls. Below him he could see Jacqui's body being moved into the waiting ambulance. He still didn't understand what she was doing out here last night. If she'd returned to her studio for her phone as Ellie Treanor had suggested, then she must have seen or heard something to make her climb up to her attic and out on to the walls, unless the phone was merely an excuse to return here, perhaps to meet someone. Just before he stepped inside the gatehouse, he noticed an electrical cable hanging down loosely. His eyes followed it along the shop roofs, but he couldn't see where it went. When he had a moment, he would ask Jimmy to check it out.

Still trying to work out Jacqui's last movements, he made his way back down the narrow steps and round the police cordon into Monk Bar Court. Mr Wang was sitting behind his counter and raised his hand when he saw Shadow, but the chocolate shop and Jacqui's place were both in darkness. Shadow tried the door of the jewellery boutique, but it was locked. He was about to leave when he heard the sound of a car engine and the beep of a horn. He turned and saw Le Vel's little red MG trying to get through the cordon. Shadow waved to the constable to let him through. The sports car rumbled over the cobbles and pulled up next to the brown vintage van. Le Vel jumped out looking full of concern.

"Hello, Chief Inspector. I've just heard about poor Jacqui from her friend Ellie. I can't quite believe it. I'm in complete shock. Any idea what happened?"

Le Vel's face was pale and serious, but in Shadow's experience people who told you they were in shock very rarely were.

"She broke her neck when she either fell or was pushed from the city walls last night. Have you any idea what she was doing out there?"

Le Vel shook his head.

"No, not at all. The last I heard she was meeting Ellie for drinks."

"May I ask where you were last night?"

"Yes certainly, I had a mad dash down to Felixstowe. After I spoke to you in the Cross Keys, I stayed for a quick pint, then I came back here only to find a consignment of chocolates I was sending to Belgium, hadn't been picked up by the courier. It was a sample selection for a new customer, who has outlets all over Europe. I didn't want to look unreliable, so I thought I'd take it myself. The boat wasn't due to sail until eleven."

"You didn't go in the van?"

"No, the van's more of a prop. It looks the part parked in front of the shop, but my car is faster—not fast enough though. I missed the boat, quite literally, by about half an hour. I suppose I'll have to fly them over now, quicker, but more expensive of course."

"I see. Why didn't the courier collect the parcel?"

"That's the strange thing, when I phoned to complain first thing this morning, they said they didn't have any record of the booking."

"That is very strange, Mr Le Vel."

Shadow did a quick calculation in his head. Felixstowe was the country's busiest container port. It was down in Suffolk and he guessed it was approximately four hours away, yet if Le Vel was only returning now, he'd been away for at least fourteen hours. As if reading his mind, Le Vel pre-empted his next question.

"Strange and a real pain. I was totally knackered after driving there, not to mention miffed that it had all been for nothing. I had to pull into a service station, Leicester Forest East on the M1, and have a kip for a few hours in the car." He rubbed the back of this neck as he twisted his head from side to side. "Not the best sleep I've ever had."

"Did you speak to anyone at Felixstowe?"

"No, there didn't seem to be any point when I knew I'd missed the boat. I did have a chat with the girl in the coffee shop at the service station. Pretty little thing."

Shadow felt his jaw tighten. This was like a boxing match. Every time he tried to land a punch, Le Vel managed to duck and weave out of the way.

"So, the chocolates never made it to Belgium?" he asked, hoping this might catch his smug opponent out.

"No," replied Le Vel as he turned and opened the small boot of his car with a slight smile. "They are still here. Do you want me to open them up for you?"

Shadow tried to ignore the feeling Le Vel was taunting

him. He leant forward and studied the large parcel. It was wrapped in brown paper with the address of somewhere in Bruges printed neatly on the label.

"No that's fine, Mr Le Vel."

"It's a shame," continued Le Vel, "but I'm sure my customer will understand." He paused and raised his hand to his mouth. "None of it seems very important now of course. I only wish I had been here for poor Jacqui. I've told the girls not to come in today. We're closing out of respect."

"Then I'll leave you to grieve in peace, Mr Le Vel. Thank you for your time."

Shadow walked slowly away from Monk Bar Court, but before he turned into Goodramgate he paused outside Mr Wang's tea shop. The open sign had rather optimistically been turned around even though it was still behind the police cordon. Inside he could see the owner, but there was no sign of his daughter. He pushed the door open.

"Good morning, Mr Wang. May I have a word?"

"Yes indeed. Is it about Miss Heaton? Lucy told me what happened." Mr Wang gestured behind him to the small kitchen where Shadow could now see Lucy singing along to the radio and mixing up some sort of concoction in a blender. Mr Wang shook his head. "It's very noisy since she returned. Why all this music and singing?" he complained. Shadow was reminded of Jacqui and her loud jazz music.

"I was just wondering if you saw anything unusual last night?"

"No, I closed the shop at five o'clock and went home. It's not far—we live on St John Street," he replied as Lucy appeared in the kitchen doorway.

"I was here until about nine o'clock, Chief Inspector, but I was busy trying out new recipes and flavours," she said. Her father gave a disapproving grunt and shuffled away into the kitchen muttering to himself in Chinese. Shadow assumed he wasn't a fan of the bubble tea either.

"Did you happen to notice anything? Maybe Miss Heaton returning or Mr Le Vel leaving?" he asked. Lucy shook her head.

"No, I didn't see Jacqui at all, but I saw Paul coming back or, to be more accurate, I saw his van. I couldn't see who was driving."

"It wasn't his MG?" asked Shadow, slightly puzzled.

"No definitely the brown van. It's got one of those old diesel engines so it's pretty noisy. I was finishing up in here when I heard it."

"It was returning, not leaving?"

"Yep."

"And what time was this?"

"Nine-ish…maybe a little before. I'd just finished clearing up, checking everything was turned off, and I was on my way out," she said.

"Right, well thank you very much, Miss Wang."

"Oh, please call me Lucy, Chief Inspector. I feel like I know you. Jimmy talks about you such a lot. You know how he likes to chat."

"Yes, he certainly does," replied Shadow with a tight smile. "Thank you again."

As he turned to leave the tea shop, he saw the red MG drive past the window. Le Vel obviously didn't want to hang around and now Shadow would have to wait to ask him who else had keys to his van. He made his way back to the station, deep in thought. As he walked down Stonegate, The Punch Bowl was opening its doors. His growling stomach reminded him that he'd missed breakfast. He glanced at his watch. It was almost lunchtime. Sophie said she wouldn't have any results until this afternoon, and they did serve a very good steak pie.

WHEN HE RETURNED to the station an hour later, Jimmy and Tom were wincing together as they watched a recording of a rugby match on Jimmy's laptop. It was a six-nations match and the French fly-half was being stretchered off after a fairly gruesome tackle, while the Scottish captain played on, despite having a heavily bandaged thigh.

"No second thoughts about playing yet, Sergeant?" Shadow asked.

"It's too late to back out now, Chief. The game is tomorrow morning. Are you coming to watch?"

"I'll see," replied Shadow watching as another French

player emerged from the scrum with a bleeding nose. "You know I'm not keen on the sight of blood. Speaking of which has Sophie been back in touch about Jacqui Heaton and did you find anything else in her attic?"

Jimmy closed his laptop and flicked open his electronic notebook instead.

"Sophie has done the post-mortem. She confirmed that it was a cervical fracture and death would have been instant. There was some alcohol in her blood, but not a particularly high level. We already know from Miss Treanor that she'd had a gin and tonic. In Sophie's opinion, the coroner will more than likely record a verdict of misadventure."

"Why?"

"Well, you see when she removed those red shoes Jacqui always wore, one of the heels felt a bit wobbly. She passed it over to Ben and Ollie. They found traces of moss on the heel and a scratch on a mossy part of the wall path above where Jacqui's body was found that looked like it could have been made by the heel so…"

"So, it sounds like her heel broke and she slipped and fell," concluded Shadow.

Jimmy nodded. "That's it, Chief."

"Right, well I still want to know what she was doing up there in the middle of the night. What else did you find in her place?"

Jimmy tapped at the screen of his notebook, to retrieve the next lot of notes.

"We got the loft hatch open and found Jacqui's bag. It was on the floor of the flat at the bottom of where the ladder that leads to the attic, comes down. She must have left it there because she needed to use two hands to help her climb the ladder steps. Ben and Ollie are still checking the bag, but there didn't seem to be anything missing. Her purse had cash and cards still in; her phone was there too. There were several missed calls from the same number. I checked, and it was Ellie Treanor's mobile number. If you remember she said she'd tried calling Jacqui after she left the bar.

"Incidentally, there were traces of blood on the loft hatch, near the scratches you spotted. Forensics checked with Sophie, but it's not Jacqui's blood. We looked around her shop and studio, but couldn't find anything out of the ordinary. It was pretty tidy, not like anything had been disturbed, but Ben spotted there wasn't a first aid kit. He thought that was strange considering Jacqui would often be working with hot metal."

"It is strange," agreed Shadow, impressed for once with his forensics team.

Jimmy carried on. "We checked the flat on the first floor, but it was completely empty."

"Any fingerprints?"

"Only Jacqui's in the flat and studio. Plenty in her shop, but that was open to the public."

"What about in the attic?"

"Well it had been cleaned pretty thoroughly, but yes Ben

and Ollie did manage to get a couple of different sets of prints. We don't know whose yet."

"Was the door between the flat and the shop locked?"

"Yes, but we couldn't find a key for it. None of Jacqui's fitted the lock."

"What about in the attic? What else did you find there?"

Jimmy started scrolling back.

"Well you already know about the hair they found. They're still running tests on that. Those burn marks on the floorboards are recent—made weeks, not months ago, by a blowtorch they think—but again more tests are being carried out. Close to the burn marks they also discovered tiny specks of gold. They are hoping they can match it to the gold to make the replica coins at the museum, but…"

"I know—awaiting more tests," interrupted Shadow impatiently.

"Yes, Chief. They also found a few grains of rice in the cracks between two of the floorboards. Most were uncooked, but a couple had been cooked, less than twenty-four hours previously according to Ben and Ollie."

"So, it looks like someone—going by the hair, possibly Ling—was there, making the fake coins, but has now been moved," said Shadow.

Jimmy nodded. "It's looking that way, Chief. Do you think Jacqui Heaton was involved?"

"Possibly. It's hard to imagine she didn't know someone was living in the attic of the place where she worked and someone must have unlocked the door into the flat for her."

"But the attic was two floors above her shop, and she did have that loud music playing all the time," reasoned Jimmy.

"As set up by Le Vel," replied Shadow.

"You back to him again, Chief?"

"I would be, but it seems he has an alibi." Shadow sighed. He briefly repeated his earlier conversation with Le Vel then turned to Tom. "Phone the Leicester Forest East service station; see if there is CCTV footage of Le Vel's MG there. It should be easy enough to spot with that personal reg. He also said he spoke to a girl who worked in one of the coffee shops; check that out too. Then when you've done that check with the bar that Ellie Treanor said she went to with Jacqui. Make sure they were there and if anyone can confirm the time Jacqui left."

"You don't trust Ellie now, Chief?" asked Jimmy looking aghast.

"Well as you have already pointed out, Sergeant, I'm suspicious by nature. Now anything else from our esteemed colleagues in the forensics department?"

"Yes, an electric cable. You see although there is an electricity supply to Jacqui's shop, because the flat above was empty, it didn't have one, but someone had run a cable into the attic; however, not up from Jacqui's shop but..."

"From Genevieve Knott's café by any chance?" interrupted Shadow again.

Jimmy looked up in surprise. "Yes, how did you know,

Chief?"

Shadow shook his head as he frowned.

"Miss Knott was complaining to me yesterday evening about her exorbitant electricity bill."

Jimmy looked slightly puzzled but kept reading what the forensics team had reported.

"Well anyway according to Ben, whoever installed the cable knew what they were doing. It looked like a pretty professional job."

SHADOW SPENT THE rest of the afternoon in his office brooding on everything that had been reported back to him. The dark clouds outside and the sleety rain battering his window suited his mood. Tom gingerly peered around his door a couple of times. First to confirm that the barman at The Botanist remembered Jacqui and Ellie arriving. They were regulars apparently. He couldn't be sure of the time, but Jacqui left first and Ellie about an hour later.

A little later, the eager young constable turned up again to inform Shadow that although the CCTV in the service station car park was broken, the young woman working night shift in the coffee shop had been tracked down and told Tom that not only was Le Vel there when he said he was but that "he was ever so charming and with such a sexy smile".

Jimmy had been despatched to break the news of Jacqui's death to her mother who was in a nursing home. As she was suffering from dementia, Shadow thought the presence of a uniformed officer might be too alarming for the poor woman. Jimmy called when he was on his way back to the station.

"How did it go?" asked Shadow.

"I'm not sure she knew who Jacqui was, let alone what I was doing there, Chief. Maybe that's a blessing."

"Maybe. By the way, do you recall which service station Ling joined the coach party at?"

"Leicester Forest East. Why?"

"That's the same one Le Vel was at last night," said Shadow, wondering if the CCTV had been working when Ling was there.

There was a long pause at the other end of the line before Jimmy finally replied.

"Even if it is, it could just be another coincidence. There are only so many service stations on the M1. You don't think you're clutching at straws, Chief?" Jimmy asked tentatively.

"Perhaps," admitted Shadow, "but right now there's nothing else to clutch on to."

A FEW HOURS later, Shadow and Jimmy left the station together. As they stepped into St Helens Square with its restaurants and bars Shadow recalled it was the fourteenth of February.

"You've been very quiet about your plans for this evening. Do I take it you have something suitably romantic organised for Sophie?" he asked.

Jimmy shook his head. "Afraid not, Chief. Sophie is busy with a post-mortem over in Harrogate and I should probably have an early night before I play rugby in the morning. It's okay though, we'll see each other at Mum's New Year party tomorrow night. Hopefully we can celebrate then. What about you, Chief?"

"I'm not taking any chances. I'm going to pick up a pizza from Gino and go straight home."

He waved his sergeant goodbye. It was the first time since he had started seeing Sophie that Shadow could recall him not having an elaborate celebration organised for a special event. Later as he sat alone in *Florence*, listening to Dean Martin with a glass of wine in his hand and an empty pizza box by his feet, Shadow thought about the day's events. Even if Sophie was right and it was ruled that Jacqui's death was misadventure, there were still plenty of unanswered questions. Who had been driving the brown chocolate van that Lucy Wang reported seeing? And what happened to the key for the door into the flat?

Then there were still the other two cases to think about. Despite what Jimmy said, he still couldn't help linking them, especially now that it looked like Ling could have been in

Jacqui's attic. All they really knew about Ling was that she was young, poor and was trained in engraving jewellery. For anyone forging coins that was a useful skill to have and whoever that was couldn't be working alone. Even if Jacqui was involved, she must have been working with someone else. Who was the other person?

Shadow returned to his idea that everyone involved in the case was part of a couple, in some instances not just one. Stephanie with her criminal connections was married to Tim Dunnington and would easily have been able to access the coins, but her loyalties seemed to lie with Pete, who in turn was rarely seen without Glen. When he'd heard the Clarkson twins talking today, he'd been reminded of the way the two ex-soldiers spoke. Almost finishing each other's sentences.

Then there was Dorothy and Genevieve, who he now knew were more than friends. Dorothy was the only other key holder to the storeroom where the coins were kept and Genevieve regularly visited China, but what was in it for them aside from financial gain? Was it possible they could be motivated purely by altruistic reasons? Did Genevieve view the poor Chinese girls in the same way she viewed the Clarkson twins or her dog Pendle? Did she think Ling and possibly Mei were in need of rescuing too?

Then as ever, he came back to Le Vel. Living in Hong Kong, his father dealing in old coins and his relationship with a jeweller, but now Jacqui was dead. Had there been a disagreement between the two of them before she died?

Shadow shook his head. He was sure Jacqui would have told Ellie if she had rowed with Paul, and Ellie hadn't mentioned anything. Jacqui had told them Le Vel had a key to the flat above her shop, but could that have been a lie? Either way, it didn't change the fact that Le Vel had an alibi.

Shadow downed the rest of his wine and yawned. Hopefully, things might seem clearer in the morning. For now, all he did know was that he'd successfully avoided another Valentine's Day and all its romantic connotations.

CHAPTER NINE

Across 9.
The cat took it and hid in the top of the house (5 letters)

S HADOW PLUNGED HIS hands into his jacket pockets and stamped his feet as he stood close to the touch line. It was Sunday morning, and it was freezing as he knew it would be. He had always thought rugby might have been more bearable if it had been played in the summer, but at least the watery winter sun was attempting to shine through the misty clouds.

There was already quite a crowd of spectators gathering to watch the match. Tom was there as well as Lucy and Angela. Jimmy had explained that it was an annual charity event. When Sophie's two brothers had been at agricultural college in York, one of their friends had been killed in a car crash. The other driver, a young army recruit at Fulford Barracks, was also killed. Since then, friends of both young men got together for a rugby match played in their memory and to raise funds for charities set up in both their names. It had become a sort of unofficial farmers versus soldiers event and as such most of the participants looked to be at least three times the width of his sergeant, who was warming up and being given a pep talk by Sophie's two brothers. Also warming up, but at the opposite end of the pitch, were Pete and Glenn. Shadow concluded that as ex-soldiers, they must have been drafted in for the army's side.

Just then there was the roar of an engine, then the screech of brakes as Stephanie arrived in her little silver sports car. She was wearing a fur hat and coat together with ridiculously high-heeled boots for the soft, muddy ground. Tottering unsteadily, she waved enthusiastically when she saw Pete stretching and lunging out on to the pitch. There was another sports car parked next to Stephanie's, a red one, and as Shadow scanned the crowd, sure enough there was Paul Le Vel laughing and joking and somehow managing to supress his grief over Jacqui's death.

Shadow watched as he shook hands, kissed cheeks and slapped backs. Only Stephanie seemed less than pleased to see him and gave Le Vel the sort of look she usually reserved for members of Her Majesty's Constabulary. Shadow also spotted Maggie wearing her green hat and coat along with a pair of bright yellow wellies. He raised his hand in greeting and with a smile, she strolled over to join him.

"Cheer up! You look like you're going to his funeral."

"It might be better for Jimmy if I was."

"Now don't be so dramatic! He'll be fine."

"I'm not sure. I think he might have a point," said a voice behind them. Shadow and Maggie turned around to

A ROMAN SHADOW

find a very tired and worried-looking Sophie standing there. She was wrapped up in a puffa coat, hat and gloves. Maggie threw her arms around her.

"Now don't listen to this doom monger. He'll be fine," she repeated. "They won't put him in the scrum and I've seen how quickly he moves when he's out jogging. He'll be able to dodge out of the way of any tackles easily."

For Sophie's sake, Shadow nodded, but still didn't feel remotely reassured and judging by Sophie's grim expression neither did she.

"What are you doing here anyway?" he asked Maggie. "I didn't have you down as a rugby fan."

"I've come to cheer on my nephew," she said nodded towards a strapping young man, who was playing for the army's team. Shadow didn't recognise him, but then Maggie came from a large family. It was almost impossible to keep track of all her cousins, nephews and nieces. At that moment the referee jogged out on to the pitch, blew his whistle and the game began.

The first half passed without any alarming incidents. Most of the action took place along the right wing and fortunately Jimmy was out of the way over on the left. Henry—Sophie's brother—scored a try first, which James— the other brother—converted. Pete and Glenn then did the same for their team. There was a slight skirmish in the scrum and the farmers' side were awarded a penalty. When the half- time whistle blew, Jimmy's team were leading by three

189

points. He gave Shadow and Sophie a thumbs up as he jogged off the pitch.

"So far so good," murmured Sophie.

Shadow kept checking his watch throughout the second half. Forty minutes had never passed so slowly. Sophie, looking slightly more relaxed, shouted encouragement to her brothers and Jimmy. To Shadow it looked like both teams were flagging, when suddenly Glenn scored a try that was swiftly converted by Pete, taking their team into the lead. Stephanie's shrieks of delight echoed across the pitch.

"Subtlety isn't the new Mrs Dunnington's strong point is it?" Maggie murmured. Shadow gave a sardonic smile and shook his head.

The change of score seemed to give Jimmy's team a new lease of life. They got hold of the ball and to Shadow's horror it was thrown out towards Jimmy, who managed to catch it. Sophie groaned and covered her face with her hands as Jimmy sprinted towards the touchline. Several opposing players were chasing him, but he dodged out of their way.

"Run!" screeched Maggie grabbing hold of Shadow's arm, as he watched his sergeant in silence. Jimmy was only a couple of feet away from scoring when Glenn closed in. Jimmy launched himself towards the touchline with the ball held out in front of him at the exact second Glenn grabbed his legs and brought him down in a vicious tackle. Glenn's head made a crunching sound as it connected with the studs on Jimmy's boot. Jimmy hit the ground heavily, but somehow managed to cling on to the ball with his fingertips as it landed just over the line. The referee blew his shrill whistle, and a cheer went up as the try was quickly converted by Sophie's brother with only seconds to spare before the referee blew his whistle again for the final time. However, both Glenn and Jimmy remained on the ground. Sophie rushed over to where Jimmy lay in the mud rubbing his head, closely followed by Shadow and Maggie. Glenn was sitting up, but blood was pouring out of a gash at his temple where he'd been cut by the spikes on Jimmy's boot. Jimmy's face was pale, but he tried getting up when he saw Sophie.

"Don't move," she ordered as she knelt down in the mud to assess him, while the referee attended to Glenn. Shadow fished his phone out of his pocket and dialled 999. As usual he was horrified at the sight of blood, but had seen enough head injuries to know that Glenn was going to need stitches.

"Did we win?" Jimmy asked weakly.

"By three points," Shadow informed him. Henry and James came running over to congratulate him, but Sophie shooed them away.

"Sit quietly," she commanded. "You might have concussion."

Jimmy obediently did as he was told while the rest of the team celebrated around him.

GLENN, UNLIKE JIMMY, was making quite a lot of noise as the stretcher he was strapped to was wheeled into the ambulance. He kept groaning and repeating "just slipped" over and over again.

"That's right, mate, you just slipped," repeated the paramedic reassuringly.

"What's wrong with him?" asked Jimmy, who still looked a little spaced out.

"He's delirious. It sometimes happens with concussion," explained Sophie.

The ambulance doors slid closed and in the darkened glass Shadow could see his own reflection and behind him the face of Paul Le Vel wearing an uncharacteristic expression. He looked worried.

After the ambulance had sped away, its sirens blaring, Shadow left Jimmy in Sophie's capable hands as she fussed over him whilst at the same times berating her brothers for involving him in the first place. Maggie was chatting to her nephew and what looked like several other members of her family, so Shadow set off on the long walk back to the city alone.

When the city walls finally came into view, the Minster was striking twelve. Shadow stepped under Bootham Bar and through the door of The Lamb and Lion. He ordered roast beef with Yorkshire puddings and a pint of Black Sheep before settling down at a small table in the window. An open fire was crackling in the grate and after a few moments he finally began to feel his numb fingers and toes again.

He enjoyed a leisurely lunch and was contemplating ordering a second pint when the short, fat tweed-clad figure of Cornelius Rutherford passed by his window. The solicitor stopped and did a double take when he spotted Shadow, who raised a hand in greeting. He was a little surprised to see the solicitor dressed formally and in the city on a Sunday, and even more surprised when a few seconds later he arrived at his table.

"Mind if I join you, Shadow?" he asked as he plonked himself down in the chair opposite.

"Not at all. Pint?" asked Shadow signalling to the barman.

"After the morning I've had can you make it a scotch?" the solicitor replied looking unusually flustered.

"Problem?"

"It's Dunnington and that damned museum. I knew I should have resigned after his divorce from Camilla. We had an emergency board meeting last night. It turns out the accounts are in an even worse state than Jonty was expecting. That combined with this theft business, well it was decided that things couldn't continue as they were. Especially since this new discovery of the Roman gladiators is going to attract a heck of a lot of attention. To put it bluntly, we can't afford any more cock-ups. We couldn't wait for Stather to return, so we, the other three members of the board, voted to remove Dunnington from his post and replace him with Dr

Shepherd."

Shadow raised an eyebrow as their drinks arrived.

"How did Dunnington take the news?"

Rutherford took a long grateful sip before continuing. "Not well, poor chap! Then about an hour ago he called me, in a bit of a state. He was over at the museum clearing his desk while nobody else was there and discovered more bad news."

"Another theft?" asked Shadow.

"Not exactly, but when he was in Stephanie's office, he came across several credit card statements. They'd all been maxed to the limit. He was a little shaken when he saw the amounts and thought he should make a start paying them off, but when he logged on to his bank accounts the joint one was empty. Completely cleared. All funds transferred into an account with a name and number he didn't recognise. He's been frantically calling Stephanie's mobile, but she's not answering. When he returned home her car and all her clothes and jewellery had gone. It looks very much like she's done a runner. I've left Jonty with him now trying to get to the bottom of things."

Shadow frowned. He had seen both Stephanie and Pete at the rugby match only a couple of hours ago, but come to think of it, he didn't recall seeing either of them when Glenn was taken away in the ambulance. Given how the two men were such close friends he did think it strange Pete wasn't there. Had he and Stephanie decided to make use of everyone being distracted by Glenn's injury to disappear?

"Does Dunnington have any idea where they might have gone?" he asked.

Rutherford shook his head. "No, he's as clueless as ever. However, when I was looking through some of the paperwork there, I found a reference for a security position out in Kuwait. It was for Pete, but Tim said he can't remember filling it in, so it looks like Stephanie might have forged his signature. If they are still in the country, I doubt they will be for long."

"And if memory serves, we don't have an extradition treaty with Kuwait," said Shadow. Rutherford took another drink and shook his head.

"You know when I first met Stephanie, I'm afraid I dismissed her as a bit of a bimbo. I thought she lacked Camilla's ability to plan and organise, but I think I might have underestimated her."

"I think you'll find you weren't the only one," Shadow agreed.

WHEN HE AND the solicitor had finished their drinks, Shadow decided to call into the station to see if any progress had been made in his absence. He sat at his desk with files for both Ling and the missing coins in front of him, but he didn't open either. He was thinking about Stephanie. They had underestimated her. She had organised events so Glenn and Pete could work at the museum. Had her motives been purely romantic or was there more to it?

Then there was Dorothy. Now she had the chance to run the museum exactly how she wanted. Was there a possibility that could have been the motive for the thefts? Maybe the coins hadn't gone anywhere; they were only taken to make Dunnington look incompetent.

Hong Kong was bothering him again too. Stephanie had visited there on her honeymoon, but it was also where Ernest Level had chosen to settle when he left York. Why had he picked that particular place? Nobody had really given an explanation. It hadn't been a British colony since 1997. Did he have ties there? Shadow recalled Maggie's comment about him having illegitimate children throughout the world. Did he have family in Hong Kong?

He was so deep in thought about Stephanie and Pete and whether they were responsible for anything more than bankrupting Dunnington that he didn't hear the knock on his door at first. The second knock was louder and accompanied by a familiar voice calling out his name.

"Yes," called out Shadow and Jimmy put his head in around the door.

"Hi, Chief, I wondered if you were here."

Shadow beckoned him in and gestured to the chair opposite him.

"What are you doing here? Shouldn't you be in hospital?"

"No, I'm fine. I had a shower and feel much better now. Sophie is dropping her brothers off at the station. They need to get back to the farm to help her dad, so I thought I'd check a couple of things back here."

Shadow told his sergeant about Pete and Stephanie.

"Shouldn't we go after them, Chief, or at least notify the airports? You've always said the innocent don't run."

"Yes, but we already know what they are guilty of and although it's morally questionable, it may not be illegal. They might not be the only ones making a run for it. Did you see Le Vel at the end of the game?"

"Chief," groaned Jimmy, "not him again!"

Before Shadow could argue. Tom appeared in the doorway looking excited and carrying a laptop.

"Sorry to interrupt, Chief Inspector Shadow, but there's something I think you should see." He turned to Jimmy and handed him the laptop. "You've had a response from the tour company, Sergeant Chang."

"What's going on?" asked Shadow, as Jimmy tapped rapidly away at the keyboard.

"I wasn't very happy with some of the responses that we got from the company organising the tour that Ling joined, so I thought I'd try making a booking under a false name and ask about joining a tour halfway through."

"I didn't tell you to do that," said Shadow.

"No, but I suppose you could say I just had a hunch,"

replied Jimmy with a smile. Shadow raised an eyebrow.

"Well it's always good to act on those," he agreed.

Jimmy started reading out loud. "Dear sir, thank you for your enquiry… Blah blah…always try and accommodate customer's needs… Blah blah." He looked up. "Sorry, Chief, false alarm, it's only a standard response," he said apologetically.

"No!" exclaimed Tom, who looked as though he was about to burst with excitement. "Look who sent it!"

Shadow moved to Jimmy's side of the desk as his sergeant scrolled down to the end of the letter. They peered at the screen and read the name at the bottom together.

"Denise Wong!"

Jimmy immediately began tapping away again, while Shadow fished his glasses out of his pocket to see more clearly.

"What are you doing now?" he asked.

"Seeing if she's on Facebook. The tour company is based in the West Midlands. There can't be that many Denise Wongs there," Jimmy explained. "Yes! Found her!" He expertly scrolled through her page. To Shadow it just looked like a blur of photos, but suddenly Jimmy stopped. "Wow!" he exclaimed turning the screen to Shadow. There was a picture of a young Chinese woman sipping a cocktail in a glamorous-looking bar. On either side of her were Glenn and Paul. The caption beneath read: 'Enjoying drinks and hanging out with my favourite brothers! Good times!'

Shadow was silent for a minute as he recalled Maggie telling him about Ernest Level's business trips to various cities that involved a lot more than coins.

"Put in a request for a copy of Glenn's birth certificate and for Denise's. Check and see if Ernest Level is definitely listed as their father," he said to Tom as he pulled on his coat. "Jimmy, come with me."

"Where to?" asked Jimmy handing the laptop back to Tom, who dashed off.

"I think I know where the girls are?"

"Where, Chief?"

"In the attic above Le Vel's shop."

"But you said you'd already looked there."

"Yes, but when I looked, they were actually next door in Jacqui's attic. When Le Vel knew I'd been poking around his place and his father's old shop, he decided to move them, thinking we wouldn't look again. I think when Jacqui returned to get her phone, she heard something, went to investigate, saw what was going on and that's when she fell."

"You don't think she was pushed then, Chief?"

"No, I'm not sure of course, but I think that's what Glenn meant when he kept saying 'just slipped' as he was put in the ambulance. He was referring to Jacqui and that's why Le Vel looked worried. He was wondering what else Glenn might say while he was delirious."

Shadow was heading out of the door, but Jimmy hadn't moved.

"Aren't you coming?" he asked.

Jimmy looked down at his feet before replying. "It's just that we still don't have a search warrant. Why not try and get one first?"

"Look, I know you are worried, but what if I'm right and Le Vel panics and tries to move the two girls again or worse gets rid of them another way? I'll take the blame, but I need you with me. I don't speak Chinese and if the girls are there, they'll be terrified if I go crashing in alone."

Jimmy nodded and with a sigh said, "Okay, let's go."

WHEN THEY ARRIVED at Monk Bar Court, the place was deserted except for Lucy and Angela sitting in the tea shop window chatting. The chocolate shop van was still parked on the cobbles, but there was no sign of Le Vel or his MG. They returned to the entrance for the city walls that was still cordoned off with police tape. Shadow ducked underneath and hauled himself up the narrow steps.

"You wait here. If I'm wrong, then you can honestly say you weren't involved," he said over his shoulder to Jimmy. He stepped out on to the city walls. There was a cold wind blowing, making the yellow police tape rattle. After a moment or two he located the crowbar Ben and Ollie had discarded the previous day. He approached the boarded-up attic window belonging to Le Vel's shop.

"Stand back," he shouted, still not sure if anybody was inside to hear him. He thrust the metal bar between the shutters. There was a crack and the wood splintered apart. Shadow stepped back. Two pairs of dark frightened eyes stared back at him. The missing girls were huddled together and were eerily quiet. He recognised the one in the pink top from her photograph.

"Ling? Mei?" he said, his voicing sounding louder than he meant it to. Ling remained silent, but as she blinked a single tear ran down her face. He racked his brain to try and remember some of the Chinese words and phrases Angela and Rose had attempted to teach him. All he could recall was *nee how* for hello and *sher sher* for thank you.

"*Nee how*," he repeated quietly and self-consciously. It didn't seem to be helping. He hurried over to the gatehouse doorway.

"Jimmy!" he bellowed down the steps. "Get up here!"

A few seconds later, his sergeant's trainer-clad feet pounded up the stairs. He stopped abruptly when he saw what Shadow had discovered.

"Oh my God, it's them," he said.

"Yes, it's them. They've been right under our noses the whole time," replied Shadow impatiently as he shifted out of the way. "Now stop staring and say something reassuring."

Jimmy knelt down so he was level with the girls' faces and began to speak to them in their own language. Shadow looked past him and the girls, and into the room. There were two mattresses on the floorboards, a small cooking stove with a saucepan and in one corner a crucible, blowtorch and other paraphernalia for making fake coins. The place was a death-trap and it must have been freezing at night. He noticed Ling's hands now covering her face in fear. They weren't old or ugly; they simply showed the signs of hard work. Shadow wasn't a violent man, but if he could have got his own hands on Le Vel right then, he'd quite happily have punched his smug face.

Neither of the girls had spoken yet. As reassuring as Jimmy might be Shadow was sure the missing girls would rather speak to a woman. After everything they'd been through, they were bound to feel that men were not to be trusted.

"I'll be back in a minute," said Shadow to his sergeant before hurrying back down through the gatehouse and down the steps. With relief he saw Angela and Lucy were both still in the tea shop. He went in and explained what had happened. The two young women immediately agreed to help and went up to join Jimmy.

Shadow telephoned the custody sergeant and asked him to send an unmarked car to Monk Bar. Then he waited impatiently on the pavement to hear what his sergeant had to report. As he paced up and down, he heard the faint sound of a violin playing. A few moments later the playing stopped, and Marco appeared from a door next to the barber's across the street and greeted him with a friendly wave.

"Hi, Chief Inspector Shadow. How are you? I've been having an extra violin lesson. I've got an exam next week."

"Well for what it's worth, it sounded good to me," replied Shadow. He thought for a second. It was a long shot, but it was worth asking. "I don't suppose you noticed a red MG leaving here while you had your lesson?"

"Paul Le Vel's MG? It's a great little car, but no sorry, I didn't see it. I did follow him on my way down here though. He was on his phone and sounded really stressed."

"Really? Can you remember what he was saying?"

"Something about leaving immediately and getting a connecting flight to Heathrow, that's all."

"That's very helpful, thank you, Marco. How do you know Mr Le Vel by the way?"

"Valentina, one of our new waitresses, used to work for him. She said he's a real slimeball." The young man looked embarrassed. "Sorry, is he a friend of yours?"

Shadow shook his head with a small smile. "No, Marco, he isn't."

"Good, well I'll be going then, Chief Inspector. See you later."

"Good luck with your exam," Shadow called after him.

No sooner had Marco walked away, than Jimmy appeared at the bottom of the steps.

"I've left Lucy and Angela talking to the girls for now, Chief."

"Did they say much to you?"

"No. They were terrified when you broke into the attic, Chief. Le Vel had convinced them that as they were here without a proper visa, if they were found they would be in a lot of trouble and sent to prison. Le Vel told them that the builders working on the empty shops were his spies and would report back if they tried to signal or shout to anyone on the walls."

"Very clever," replied Shadow sarcastically. "The builders were also useful for masking any noise the girls may have made too. Did they say if Le Vel or Glenn had physically hurt them in any way?"

"No, but to be honest, Chief, they didn't say a lot. I tried to reassure them, but they were frightened to talk to me. Maybe Angela and Lucy will have more luck with them."

"Do they speak any English?"

"Not much I don't think. It seems Le Vel spoke to them in Chinese."

Shadow thought for a moment, then instructed his sergeant to begin contacting the Chinese authorities. Shadow himself phoned the custody sergeant again to ask him to prepare one of the custody suites and ensure there was a female doctor on site when he brought the two girls in.

LESS THAN AN hour later and they were all back at the station. Shadow waited up in the incident room while the doctor spoke to Ling and Mei. He paced up and down while Jimmy and Tom were both busy making telephone calls. Jimmy was the first to report back to him.

"Sorry, Chief, but nobody from the Chinese embassy can get up here until tomorrow with it being our New Year and everything."

"Fine," replied Shadow, "they'll have to stay here I suppose."

Before Jimmy could say any more his phone bleeped loudly. He excused himself and hurried downstairs. At the same time Tom finished his call.

"I've just had confirmation, sir," said Tom. "Ernest Level is named as the father on Glenn Denton's birth certificate. Denise Wong was born in Hong Kong, so we haven't been able to check her yet."

"No, but it would make sense if Ernest moved there, to be near his daughter. Now we know Le Vel is definitely Glenn's half-brother, send a couple of officers to the hospital to guard him. Tell them to let us know immediately if Le Vel turns up."

Tom picked up the phone again and Jimmy returned waving several pieces of paper.

"I've been down to see Angela, Chief. She's taken notes of everything Mei and Ling told her and Lucy."

Shadow nodded appreciatively and held out his hand, then noticing the papers were all covered in Chinese characters sighed.

"You'd better translate, Sergeant."

Jimmy scanned through the papers.

"Both Mei and Ling confirmed that they travelled using Denise Wong's passport. Le Vel told them it would be easier as it's a BNO one."

"And of course then they'd be over here without any papers and completely reliant on him," snorted Shadow.

"They both said he was kind and charming when he first met them, but totally changed when he got them in the attic."

Shadow paused, dreading the answer to his next question.

"Any signs of abuse?"

Jimmy clicked on the medical report that had been emailed up to him.

"No, Mei has lost quite a lot of weight and both are a little dehydrated, but otherwise okay."

Shadow let out a huge sigh of relief.

"Oh, Ling has a cut on her hand," Jimmy added. "She got it trying to claw through the loft hatch. Glenn got her a plaster for it, but the doctor has cleaned it up properly."

"If Glenn got the plaster from Jacqui's first aid kit, maybe that's why the door between the shop and flat was unlocked. It's what led Jacqui to investigate what was going on when she returned unexpectedly," said Shadow. "Have either Ling or Mei talked about how they got to York?"

"They were both given tickets for the tour. I don't think

Le Vel wanted to risk anyone seeing him bring them in. Everything went okay with Mei, but Ling's flight was delayed, which meant he had to collect her and then drop her off at the service station. They were both told to meet him again on the city walls."

"That sounds like we'll be able to charge the real Denise Wong too. What about Glenn?"

"They said he brought the coins to Le Vel and that he helped move them from the attic above Jacqui's."

"Did they see what happened to Jacqui?"

"No, but they both heard a scream. It really frightened them. I don't get it, Chief. I thought Le Vel was in Felixstowe that night."

"He needed us to think that. He knew I suspected him because I'd searched his place. I think he drove his MG out of the city, then came back, moved the girls and got Glenn to drive him out in the van to collect his car. Lucy saw Glenn coming back. With Jacqui finding them, then falling, it was even more important that he had an alibi, so he drove to the service station, made sure he spoke to someone and came up with the story about going to Felixstowe. And why on earth is your phone bleeping constantly?"

Jimmy pulled his phone out of his pocket, looking apologetic.

"Sorry, Chief, I'll put it on vibrate. I let Mrs Chen know that we'd found Ling. She was really pleased and said it was an auspicious start to the New Year. Now the rest of the tour party is texting to congratulate me and wish me a happy New Year."

"I see, now if we can get back to the case. Did Mei and Ling talk about replicating the coins?"

"Oh yes, Mei had done most of the work obviously. It seemed the coins were such a success that Le Vel wanted to start coping jewellery, not realising the theft was about to be discovered. That's why he needed Ling to help and to increase the output, so to speak. Apparently if Le Vel didn't think they worked quickly enough or didn't do a good job, he withheld food. Angela is getting Mum to bring them something to eat from the restaurant. They are both starving."

"Do either of them know where he is now?"

Jimmy leafed through his sister's notes again.

"No, he brought them some food last night, but they haven't seen him since. However, Mei said she thinks he sends the coins out hidden in boxes of chocolates and they are flown out, from Leeds Bradford."

Shadow reached for his jacket and pulled it on while thanking his lucky stars that both Angela and Lucy had been available to speak to the Chinese girls. They would never have found out all this information without them. He turned to Tom, who was waiting expectantly with pencil poised.

"Contact Inspector Grabowski at the NCA and tell her everything we know. If you need us, we'll be at Leeds Bradford Airport. Phone them too and tell them to stop Le

Vel if he tries to board a flight, probably to Heathrow," he ordered.

"Are we going now, Chief?" queried Jimmy.

"No, a week on a Friday, Sergeant. Of course now!" he replied irritably.

Jimmy shifted uncomfortably and looked down at his feet. "It's just that there's the party tonight, Chief."

"Then you had better not waste any more time here complaining," snapped Shadow as he headed out of the door.

CHAPTER TEN

Down 3.
A sweet treat so why does Lucy hate Coco? (9 letters)

THE AIRPORT WAS only about an hour away from York. While Jimmy drove, Shadow received a phone call to let him know Glenn would be in hospital for at least another twenty-four hours, but a police guard had been placed on the door of his room and as yet, he hadn't received any visitors.

"When do you think the first theft took place, Chief?" asked Jimmy.

"I'd say about three months ago, when Mei left Shanghai and Le Vel or rather Glenn tapped into Genevieve's electricity. Remember Jake told me he was in logistics in the army. Running a cable across would have been quite easy for him. But I think Le Vel set about planning the whole thing as soon as he heard his half-brother had a security job at the museum. He charmed Jacqui and encouraged her to move to Monk Bar Court. With the lease for that property in her name and the electricity coming from Genevieve, he could hide the girls there without anyone connecting the property to him."

When they arrived at the airport, they immediately noticed several police cars with flashing blue lights were already there. Half a dozen uniformed officers were standing together, and a cordon had already been put around the red MG.

"What's going on?" Shadow asked the nearest uniformed sergeant, after introducing himself and explaining why they were there.

"I'm sorry, sir, you'll have to wait if you want to speak to Mr Le Vel. He's already been arrested by Inspector Grabowski. She was acting on a tip-off."

"Yes, a tip-off from one of my constables. I asked him to phone the airport and the NCA," replied Shadow in exasperation. He couldn't believe they had driven over here and found Le Vel but were not going to be allowed to question him. The sergeant checked through his notes.

"No, sir, it was from a Mrs Stephanie Dunnington. She left her phone number in case there was a reward."

Despite his irritation, Shadow also begrudgingly had a feeling of respect for Stephanie. It seemed they really had underestimated her. Although frustrated he wasn't able to arrest Le Vel himself, Shadow took great satisfaction in watching him being taken into custody by Saskia Grabowski, who was clearly completely immune to his charms.

"Inspector, please, I beg of you. Just give me a moment to explain. I'm sure I can help you see that this is all a terrible misunderstanding," Le Vel protested, treating Inspector Grabowski to one of his most charming smiles.

She was unmoved. "Shut it, sunshine! I don't need any help understanding people smuggling when I see it, especially not from scum like you," she replied, placing her hand on Le Vel's handsome blond head and shoving him none too delicately into the back of a waiting police car.

As Le Vel was driven away, Inspector Grabowski came over to speak to Shadow.

"I'm sorry, sir, but we came straight here when we got the tip-off."

"No need to apologise, Inspector. We have his accomplice and his two victims back in York should you need to speak with them."

"Thank you, sir. I understand you are also investigating a theft of Roman coins."

"Yes, how do you know?"

"That was part of the tip-off too. We found several of them hidden in a shipment of chocolates bound for China. Our forensics team have them at the moment, but I'll ensure they are returned to you."

Shadow nodded. Mei had been right. He thanked the inspector and with a sigh he and Jimmy walked back to their car.

"Why did Stephanie shop him?" asked Jimmy.

"I think she worked out before any of us what was going on. Glenn was taking the coins while she and Pete were, how shall I put it, otherwise engaged and dropping them off somewhere along the wall for Le Vel to collect and copy. I don't think Pete was involved, but Stephanie knew he could be implicated, and she wasn't prepared to see another man she loves end up in jail like her father. Phoning the NCA also had the extra benefit of ensuring North Yorkshire Police, the force responsible for putting her father away, won't be able to take the credit for arresting Le Vel."

"No, Chief, but at least we rescued Ling and Mei. That's the main thing."

Shadow grunted. He knew his sergeant was right, but still he would have enjoyed putting those handcuffs on Le Vel himself. When they reached their car, Shadow glanced over to Jimmy. His sergeant was looking paler by the minute.

"Give me the keys, Sergeant. You look terrible."

"But you don't drive, Chief," protested Jimmy.

"I may choose not to, but that doesn't mean I'm not capable. Now hand them over."

Reluctantly, Jimmy gave him the keys and slid into the passenger seat. Shadow took his place behind the steering wheel. Despite his confident declaration, he still needed to take a deep breath as he turned the ignition. It was over twenty-five years since he'd been behind the wheel.

On their journey back to York, Shadow doggedly stuck to the speed limit and remained in the slow lane of the motorway, ignoring the honking of frustrated trucks as they overtook him. However, there wasn't so much as a sigh from his sergeant. Instead he sat in silence staring out of the window. Shadow didn't think he'd ever known him to be so quiet for so long. He wasn't even humming or whistling under his breath as he normally did.

"Are you feeling all right, Sergeant? You don't have much to say for yourself today," he asked, wondering if he should drop Jimmy straight off at the hospital for a check-up. That blow to the head might have been worse than they thought.

"I'm okay, Chief, I've just got a lot on my mind," replied Jimmy as he continued to gaze out of the window. Fighting every instinct he possessed, Shadow cleared his throat.

"Anything you feel the need to talk about?" he asked fervently hoping to receive a negative answer. It was with a huge amount of relief that he saw Jimmy give a small shake of his head.

"Thanks, Chief, but I think it's probably too late for any advice."

"That sounds ominous," murmured Shadow.

A trace of a smile crossed Jimmy's lips. "No it's okay, Chief. It's just something I need to sort out myself."

Shadow nodded in what he hoped was an understanding manner and let the matter drop.

THEY ARRIVED BACK in York with less than an hour to spare until the start of Rose's party to celebrate the Chinese New

Year. The two detectives hurried down Goodramgate together. It was a clear crisp evening.

"Do you think it might snow, Chief?" asked Jimmy.

"It certainly feels cold enough to. Why?"

"I just thought it would be nice. You know more special."

"Not if you have to walk or drive in it," complained Shadow.

They arrived at the door of The Golden Dragon, but Jimmy didn't stop.

"Where are you off to?" asked Shadow.

"To see Lucy. She's making the fortune cookies," Jimmy called back over his shoulder as he jogged down towards the Wangs' tea shop. Shadow stepped through the doors and approached the stairs to the main part of the restaurant only to find Tom balancing precariously on top of a stepladder Angela was clinging on to. The young constable was hanging red bunting marked with Chinese symbols along the old wooden rafters.

"What are you doing here?"

"I invited him, Chief Inspector," replied Angela. "Tom was very helpful and kind when Lucy and I were talking to Ling and Mei. Also, with Jimmy away I needed someone tall to help put up the decorations. The symbol means good fortune. How do we say that in Chinese, Tom?"

"*Fu*," replied Tom obediently, "and *gung hay fat choi* is happy New Year."

"Very good," praised Angela, clearly delighted. She may have left the classroom behind for the day, but she never stopped being a teacher. Shadow was relieved that now she had another pupil, she was too distracted to make him repeat the phrase as she usually did. Just then Shadow felt someone tap him on the shoulder. When he turned around, he found Jimmy's grandfather waiting for him, holding the backgammon board. New Year or no New Year celebrations, he wasn't going to miss out on his weekly game with Shadow. The two adversaries settled in an alcove behind the kitchen out of the way of Rose and her staff. As ever Shadow was soundly beaten and as Jimmy's grandfather removed his last piece from the board, Rose shouted down the stairs to them.

"What are you both doing down there? Come upstairs. We are almost ready to begin the meal," she called impatiently, first in English and then Chinese. Shadow and his opponent exchanged a glance before obediently doing as they were told.

Upstairs, the restaurant was buzzing with people. Shadow looked around the room. He knew almost everyone there. Mr Wang was chatting to Genevieve and Dorothy, while Sophie was listening to Gino tell a joke, as Rose dashed around making last-minute adjustments. Shadow was shocked to see Ling and Mei were there too, sitting together looking a little shy.

"What are they doing here?" Shadow hissed to Tom, who was now busy folding napkins. The young constable looked a little embarrassed.

"I'm not really sure, sir. The doctor said they were okay then Mrs Chang arrived at the station with some food for them and invited them here. Sergeant Hedley said it didn't seem right keeping them down in the custody suite and, well, with it being their New Year and everything... Mrs Chang made it sound like us being stuck in a police station on Christmas Eve and as they hadn't done anything wrong it did seem unfair, so Sergeant Hedley said it would be okay to let them come along. After all you and Sergeant Chang would be here."

Shadow tutted loudly and shook his head. This was typical of George. He had two daughters himself and family was everything to him. Shadow knew full well he would have hated the idea of the two young women, who had been through such a lot, missing out on an important celebration when they were miles away from home. He was too kindhearted for his own good sometimes.

"If one of them goes missing again and there's a diplomatic incident with China because of this, Constable, I'll be holding you personally responsible," he grumbled before wandering over to a board in the corner where Rose had pinned a seating plan. She and her team of waiters and waitresses had, remarkably quickly, managed to rearrange the tables into a large U-shape after the last of the lunchtime customers had left. Shadow found his seat. He had been placed between Maggie and Maria from Catania's. That at least was something. He wouldn't be required to do much talking with the two of them on either side of him.

Maggie arrived a few moments later, slightly out of breath having hauled her suitcase up the stairs. Like Rose and Angela, she was wearing a red dress beneath her winter coat, which she took off and draped over her chair after wheeling the suitcase under the table and out of the way.

"You are definitely going to Spain then?" asked Shadow.

"Yes, I've booked on to a flight that leaves from Leeds early tomorrow morning. Twelve hours from now, I intend to be on the beach soaking up the sun and sipping sangria."

"You certainly deserve it after everything you've been through," said Shadow as he poured them both a glass of wine from the bottle on the table.

"I hear you've had quite the dramatic day too! Breaking down doors to rescue damsels in distress." Maggie nodded over to where Mei and Ling were sitting on either side of Jimmy's grandfather. He seemed to be telling them a story. Shadow had never seen the old man look so animated. "Seriously though," continued Maggie, "are they both okay?"

"The doctor says so. I expected being here surrounded by people who speak their own language and knowing they'll soon be home must help." Shadow paused and took a sip of his wine. "But heaven knows if they will experience any long-term psychological effects."

Maggie shook her head.

"If Paul Le Vel were here right now, I'd wring his neck. I

thought he was just a harmless charmer, but you saw through him. You never took to him, did you?"

"No but I don't always get it right either. The other afternoon, I shouldn't have implied you were nosy and a gossip. I know you just take an interest in other people because you care."

"My goodness, have you been working on that apology?" asked Maggie with a grin.

"Only for the last couple of days," admitted Shadow.

"Well it was pretty good for you."

"Thanks."

When everyone had taken their seats and the appetisers of spring rolls were being served, Shadow noticed there was an empty place at the end of one of the tables.

"Someone hasn't turned up," he said quietly to Maggie. She turned to look where he was pointing.

"No, they do that on purpose. Rose always sets a place for her late husband."

ROSE HAD LAID on nothing short of a banquet for her guests and the room was soon alive with the sound of everyone chatting and enjoying the delicious food. Everyone that was except Jimmy. Shadow wasn't the only one to notice.

"You have barely touched your food!" Rose chided her son. "Are you ill?"

Sophie looked worried too.

"Maybe we should take you in for a CT scan. You are really quiet," she said.

"No, I'm fine," Jimmy tried to reassure them, but he still looked pale and drawn. Shadow watched his sergeant for a moment and saw him glance nervously over to Lucy. In return she gave Jimmy an encouraging smile, which made Shadow feel quite uneasy.

The final course of the meal was coffee, or tea for those who preferred it, accompanied by the fortune cookies Lucy had made. Angela served the hot drinks while Jimmy handed out the cookies. Maggie opened her cookie first.

"Ooo mine's very accurate: 'a new, exciting and unexpected journey awaits'. That must be my trip to Spain," she declared.

Shadow broke into his. It read, 'If the fates seem to be against you, they probably are'. He raised an eyebrow.

"Yes, mine sounds about right too."

Suddenly Sophie gave an uncharacteristic squeal as she opened her cookie and read what was inside. At the same time Jimmy dropped to one knee in front of her and produced a ring box from his pocket.

"Yes!" Sophie gasped as she flung her arms around his neck. "Of course I'll marry you!"

Lucy and her father whooped and applauded, as Maria let out a gasp of excitement. Angela ran over to hug the happy couple and Rose dabbed furiously at her eyes with a napkin. Shadow suddenly felt a sharp pain in his ankle. He turned to look at Maggie who was wearing a fixed grin while at the same time nodding her head meaningfully at him.

"Did you just kick me?" he hissed. "What was that for?"

"Stand up and say something," she hissed back. "Something nice."

"Why?" he asked in a whisper, horrified at the thought of making a speech to a room full of people. He avoided any sort of public speaking whenever possible. It was one thing to address an incident room during an investigation—that was bad enough—but he had absolutely no experience of speaking at this sort of family occasion.

"Because Angela and Rose are both in tears and Jimmy's grandfather doesn't speak any English," Maggie whispered back. Shadow looked around the room. With a sinking feeling, he realised that as usual she was right. Sophie and Jimmy deserved a proper response. It was going to be torture. It was the very situation he'd tried so hard to avoid all week. Best get it over with quickly. Taking a deep breath, he rose to his feet and tapped a spoon against the side of his glass.

"Ladies and gentlemen, if I could have your attention just for a moment." He felt everyone's eyes on him, looking up expectantly. His mouth felt dry, but he ploughed on. "Firstly, I'd like to thank Rose, not only for the delicious meal we have all enjoyed, but also for including us in a celebration that is so special to her family. Of course we didn't know quite how special tonight would turn out to be," he said nodding towards a beaming Jimmy and Sophie. He paused and his eyes flicked across to the seat left empty for Jimmy's father. It should have been him here congratulating his son. Life could be very cruel, he thought as he carried on speaking. "Earlier, Angela explained to me that the decorations we see all around us are to wish good fortune for the coming year. I dare say, like me, everyone here has experienced their fair share of fortune good and bad, things in our life we are grateful for, others that we wish had turned out differently. Although I may not have been blessed with a family of my own, I have been lucky enough to have two special young people come into my life. Sophie with her intelligence, sense of humour and ability to remain calm in any crisis and Jimmy with his kind heart, unfailing optimism and perhaps most luckily for me, his tolerance of others. So, on behalf of everyone here, I'd like to wish you both health, happiness and above all good fortune in the years ahead. I can't think of a more deserving couple." He raised his glass. "To Jimmy and Sophie."

"Jimmy and Sophie," echoed the rest of the room as they then broke into spontaneous applause. Sophie and Jimmy flung their arms around each other. Shadow sat down with relief and turned to Maggie whose eyes were glistening with tears as she clapped.

"Was that all right?" he asked.

"Very nice," she replied as she sniffed and raised a tissue

to her eyes. Shadow suddenly felt an arm around his neck as Maria, with tears streaming down her face, planted a very wet kiss on his cheek.

"You are a lovely man! That was a lovely speech!" She kissed him again before standing up and hurrying over to embrace the happy couple.

"Well, you're full of surprises. I didn't know you had it in you," said Maggie quietly. Shadow wiped Maria's lipstick off his cheek and straightened his tie.

"Good. I'd hate you to think I was predictable."

"Well, I certainly don't anymore," she replied with a smile.

After that, everything went a bit mad. Gino disappeared to his own restaurant and returned laden down with bottles of champagne. Jimmy's grandfather put his favourite Elvis CD on the stereo and before long, half the room was dancing along to 'Blue Suede Shoes'. Shadow sipped his champagne and watched as Gino twirled Maria around while Maggie and a surprisingly light-footed Mr Wang danced together. Genevieve and Dorothy performed a complicated but perfectly coordinated hand jive routine much to the delight of Ling and Mei. Jimmy slipped into the empty seat next to him. The colour had returned to his face as had his usual grin. Shadow offered him his hand.

"Congratulations."

"Thanks, Chief, and thank you for everything you said. It really meant a lot to me and Sophie."

"You're welcome. I would say any time, but I'm hoping you're not going to make a habit of getting engaged."

Jimmy looked serious for a second.

"No, I can promise you this is the one and only time. I'll never find another Sophie. Besides the stress of planning it nearly killed me. I wasn't sure Ellie would have the ring ready on time. Then my first idea was to have Lucy put the ring in a fortune cookie, but she thought it might get damaged, so we hid my proposal in there instead, but I've been having nightmares about it going to the wrong person. Then all day today I kept thinking about what I'd do if she said no." Shadow glanced over to where Sophie was excitedly showing Lucy her ring. He didn't think her answer was ever in doubt. "So I'm sorry if I've been a bit quiet these last few days," Jimmy added, "and sorry for giving you such a hard time about Le Vel. You were right about him all along. I should have supported you, Chief."

"We all make mistakes," replied Shadow a little ungraciously. In truth, it was only now that he could admit even to himself, that he'd been suspicious of Jimmy's actions. He'd doubted him when it turned out that the secret meetings and conversations with Lucy had been about nothing more than fortune cookies. He should have had more faith in his sergeant, the most honest person he knew.

"I hated keeping a secret from everyone too," continued Jimmy, who now he had begun unburdening himself, clearly couldn't stop. "Sophie thought I was being weird. I had to keep sneaking around behind her back. Then I had to come up with an excuse when she caught me going through her jewellery box to try and find her ring size for Ellie. Then with Jacqui dying I thought Ellie might be too upset to finish it. I kept wanting to ask your advice, but then I worried that you'd probably tell me to wait."

Shadow thought for a moment. One of his greatest regrets was that he hadn't proposed to Luisa. He'd wanted to of course, but he'd kept waiting for the right time: when he'd passed his exams to be a sergeant, or she'd graduated. His head had ruled his heart.

He shook his head as he replied to his sergeant. "I'd have done no such thing. If experience and years of working in the police has taught me anything, it's that life is short. If you are lucky enough to find the right person, don't waste a second."

"Sorry, Chief, I guess I underestimated you," apologised Jimmy.

Shadow looked over to where Maggie was now doing the twist to 'Jailhouse Rock'.

"Yes, well apparently you aren't the only one."

Shadow drained his glass of champagne, patted his sergeant on the back and went to offer Sophie his congratulations.

A LITTLE AFTER midnight, Shadow and Maggie stood outside the Golden Dragon waiting for the taxi to take her to the airport. Back inside the restaurant the party was still in full swing.

"So, did you mean what you said earlier?" asked Maggie swaying slightly. She was still flushed and a little giddy from the champagne. Shadow frowned. It had been a long night.

"Which bit?"

"About not being lucky enough to have a family of your own. Do you feel like you've missed out?"

The furrows on Shadow's brow deepened. In truth, he'd spoken instinctively. There hadn't been time to plan what he was going to say.

"They do say you don't miss what you've never had, but sometimes on occasions like tonight, I suppose I do wonder what life could have been like if things had worked out differently. If I'd taken a different course."

"It's not too late you know," replied Maggie gently. Shadow shook his head ruefully.

"Of course, it is! I'm far too old to have children," he scoffed.

This time it was Maggie's turn to shake her head. "I didn't mean children, John. I meant it's not too late for your life to take a different course. If you want it to."

Shadow stared at her for a second, but before he could say anything in response, the taxi pulled up to the kerb. Shadow opened the car door for her and helped the driver load the luggage into the boot.

"You really don't believe in travelling light do you?" he commented as he heaved in the heavy suitcase.

"I'm following my Girl Guide training—'be prepared'." She giggled and gave a wobbly three-fingered salute as he helped her inside.

"Don't worry, she'll probably sleep most of the way," said Shadow to the grinning taxi driver. "Just make sure she's okay at the other end, will you?"

"No problem. Sam's an old mate from school. I'll take good care of Mrs J," the driver replied.

As the taxi pulled away the rear window was wound down and Maggie leaned out.

"*Adios!*" she called out loudly and blew him a kiss before ducking back inside. Shadow smiled as he waved her good-bye. He stood for a moment and watched the taxi disappear beneath Monk Bar. Then he turned and began walking towards the river. The moon slipped out from behind a cloud, casting his shadow behind him, as the first few flakes of snow fluttered to the ground.

THE END

Want more? Check out John Shadow's latest case in
A Ghostly Shadow!

Join Tule Publishing's newsletter for more great reads and weekly deals!

A ROMAN SHADOW – CROSSWORD

1.			2.		3.		/////	/////	/////
	/////	/////		/////		/////	4.	/////	/////
	/////	/////		/////		/////		/////	5.
	/////	/////		/////	6.				
	/////	7.	/////	/////		/////		/////	
8.							/////	/////	
/////	/////		/////	/////		/////	/////	/////	
/////	/////		/////	9.					/////
/////	/////		/////	/////		/////	/////	/////	/////
/////	/////		/////	/////	/////	/////	/////	/////	/////

Across

1. Good lip care ensures you won't look like a fake (7 letters)
6. Slowly inch a step towards this country (5 letters)
8. Using legs and gum you cannot legally get across the border (7 letters)
9. The cat took it and hid in the top of the house (5 letters)

Down

1. Norman lost the North so took the South route to find some Italians (6 letters)
2. Gertrude, Imogen, Nancy and Laura are initially not as popular as the girl from Shanghai (4 letters)
3. A sweet treat so why does Lucy hate Coco? (9 letters)
4. A pound, euro or dime to pay in company partly (4 letters)
5. This structure stopped them all going South or West (5 letters)
7. Will mum use this building to inspire and educate? (6 letters)

A ROMAN SHADOW – SOLUTION

1. R	E	P	2. L	I	3. C	A	/////	/////	/////
O	/////	/////	I	/////	H	/////	4. C	/////	/////
M	/////	/////	N	/////	O	/////	O	/////	5. W
A	/////	/////	G	/////	6. C	H	I	N	A
N	/////	7. M	/////	/////	O	/////	N	/////	L
8. S	M	U	G	G	L	E	/////	/////	L
/////	/////	S	/////	/////	A	/////	/////	/////	S
/////	/////	E	/////	9. A	T	T	I	C	/////
/////	/////	U	/////	/////	E	/////	/////	/////	/////
/////	/////	M	/////	/////	/////	/////	/////	/////	/////

If you enjoyed *A Roman Shadow,*
you'll love the next book in…

THE CHIEF INSPECTOR SHADOW SERIES

ABOUT THE AUTHOR

H L Marsay always loved detective stories and promised herself that one day, she would write one too. She is lucky enough to live in York, a city full of history and mystery. When not writing, the five men in her life keep her busy – two sons, two dogs and one husband.

Thank you for reading

A Roman Shadow

If you enjoyed this book, you can find more from all our great authors at TulePublishing.com, or from your favorite online retailer.

TULE
PUBLISHING

Printed in Great Britain
by Amazon

81577223R00141